PROJECT SUPERHERO

WRITTEN BY E. PAUL ZEHR   ILLUSTRATED BY KRIS PEARN

ECW PRESS

Published by ECW Press
2120 Queen Street East, Suite 200, Toronto, Ontario, Canada M4E 1E2
416-694-3348 / info@ecwpress.com

This is a work of fiction. Names, characters, places, and incidents either are the product of
the author's imagination or are used fictitiously, and any resemblance to actual persons, living
or dead, business establishments, events, or locales is entirely coincidental.

LIBRARY AND ARCHIVES CANADA CATALOGUING IN PUBLICATION

Zehr, E. Paul, author
Project superhero / E. Paul Zehr ; illustrator, Kris Pearn.

For ages 8-12.
ISBN 978-1-77041-180-7
Also issued as 978-1-77090-591-7 (pdf)   978-1-77090-590-0 (epub)
I. Pearn, Kris, illustrator   II. Title.

PS8649.E465P76 2014   jC813'.6   C2014-902550-5
C2014-902551-3

Editor: Patricia Ocampo
Cover design and all interior images: © Kris Pearn
Interior layout and design: Rachel Ironstone

This book was printed in July 2014
at Edwards Brothers–Malloy in Ann Arbor, MI, USA
1   2   3   4   5

The publication of *Project Superhero* has been generously supported by the Canada Council
for the Arts, which last year invested $157 million to bring the arts to Canadians throughout
the country. We acknowledge the support of the Ontario Arts Council (OAC), an agency
of the Government of Ontario, which last year funded 1,793 individual artists and 1,076
organizations in 232 communities across Ontario, for a total of $52.1 million. We also
acknowledge the financial support of the Government of Canada through the Canada Book
Fund for our publishing activities, and the contribution of the Government of Ontario through
the Ontario Book Publishing Tax Credit and the Ontario Media Development Corporation.

For Andi, Ani, Emma, and Jordan

MONDAY, SEPTEMBER 8
The first day of my diary.
Or first entry. Or whatever.

Grade 8 is already crazier than I imagined it would be.
That's why I started this diary — to keep track of all
the craziness. But I think it's going to be fun. I really
like writing: it's like thinking out loud but in a quiet way.
I think maybe I'll be an author or a journalist when I get
older. Or maybe a scientist. Something where I can ask
questions and get answers!

But of all the questions I have, my main one is this: why
are all the homework assignments and projects coming
up already? Didn't the teachers get the memo that it's
still only the first week of school?

I wish we were kind of "easing into" the year. Maybe
gradually introduce some homework as we go along.
Like, say, after Halloween or perhaps even later. I'm
very flexible on the "later," just as long as it IS later. It
could be as late as March break.

Lots of questions are being asked, and asked too
soon, in my humble opinion. (Which I guess isn't all that
humble, since I think I'm right.) But seriously, this early
into the year should we really have expected questions
like, "Who are you anyway?" and "Who do you want to
be?"

Here's an example from Socials today. Which again, just in case it was unclear, was day 1 of grade 8.

Ms. King, my friendly neighborhood homeroom supervisor and Socials teacher, was giving us some "food for thought" (her words).

"This year we are going to explore what it means to be a hero. What characteristics do heroes have? What does it take to be a hero? Are heroes born, or are they made? What's the difference between a hero and superhero? And why is our culture so interested in superheroes?"

To which I shot up my hand and answered, "Um . . . obviously because superheroes are way cool!" I didn't say that actually, and I didn't shoot up my hand. I just thought about doing it.

I was so busy thinking about what I might have said that I almost missed the big announcement.

The big thing is this:

WE ARE DOING A PROJECT ABOUT SUPERHEROES!

She called it the "Superhero Slam"! And guess who's into superheroes and superhero comics — me! How awesome is grade 8 going to be? Really awesome . . . except for all the homework.

Ms. King went on for quite some time. She was in that teacher-on-a-roll mode. She's pretty great so far, and I actually like her. But I had gone off daydreaming about superheroes. I've read just about every superhero comic book and seen all the movies. But I've never really thought about why I like them in the first place. And why they might be important.

I started to think about superheroes in a new way. Like I always wondered if Spider-Man would have still been a hero without his Spidey sense. And although I think he's a great character, is Batman really a superhero? He doesn't actually have any superpowers. I guess I'll get a chance to look into this in detail because we all have to choose a superhero and then argue that our superhero is the best! Cool!

Ms. King promised to tell us more about the project tomorrow.

I was still super excited when I walked home from the bus stop with my little sister, Shay. But I didn't call her "little sister" today. I wanted to walk home in peace.

And in one piece. We go to different schools but we sometimes wind up on the same bus.

After we got home, we both went to our rooms and closed our doors for homework time. Not sure why we close the doors all the time, but we get our own space that way, I guess! Since nobody else was home, we got along fine. We try to save our sisterly fights for an appreciative audience.

That's not to say Shay didn't try to provoke me. I finally told her about the Superhero Slam and how excited I was. All she did was give me that look that sisters give sisters when they are trying to annoy them and kind of mumbled "whatever." Today I was in such a good mood I just ignored her. Then when Mom and Dad both got home from work, I didn't want to waste any time on fighting with Shay.

I was so eager to tell my parents about the Superhero Slam that I almost couldn't talk when I went running into the kitchen to give them the lowdown.

Me: "Mom, Dad! SchoolwasawesometodayWehave abigprojectthatisallaboutsuperheroesIt'scalledthe SuperheroSlamIcannotbelieveitSuperheroesaremy thingHowcoolisthat?!"

Dad: "Um. What did you say?"

Mom: "Did you say something about superheroes?"

Dad: "And slamming something?"

Me (after taking a big breath and sitting down): "OK. Mom. Dad. School was awesome today. We have a big project that is all about superheroes! It's called the Superhero Slam. I cannot believe it! Superheroes are my thing! How cool is that!"

While I was getting that all out, I couldn't help noticing Shay — Little Miss Whatever — peeking around the corner listening in and looking very interested.

SISTERS.

After hearing me ramble on a bit more, Mom and Dad suggested I try to organize my thoughts somehow. Dad said this diary would be a good place to write down my plan and what might be needed to get things done. Since he's a writer and I think I got the "details gene" from him, this seems like a good idea! Mom said she could help me with anything science-y that I need. Helps to have a physiology professor for a mom!

This whole plan is right up my alley! It's also good practice for trying out the whole journalist thing. When I think about it, lots of superhero stories and superhero

11

alter egos involve reporters and writers.

Clark Kent is a journalist when he isn't busy being Superman. Or even when he is, really. And, with Spider-Man, Peter Parker isn't a journalist exactly, but he does take pictures that writers use in their DAILY BUGLE stories.

I just finished reading this cool story arc in DAREDEVIL: END OF DAYS where Ben Urich, a writer for the DAILY BUGLE, riffs on some classic SPIDER-MAN.

Ben is talking to his son. When his son says, "You're a reporter," Ben replies, "A journalist. There is a lot of power in that. I write something about someone . . . those words have power . . . with that power comes a lot of . . . of . . . of . . ." and then his son chimes in with "responsibility."

Classic SPIDER-MAN: "With great power comes great responsibility."

Like I said, I'm pretty sure I want to be a writer or journalist. Being a journalist means having lots of power, since you can influence people's opinions with what you report, and that comes with responsibility too, for sure, which seems so cool. But the biggest reason I want to be a journalist is I really like listening to people's stories. (Probably that's why I loved to listen to Gramma so much! She told stories like no one else.)

The tricky part for me is you have to ask questions as a journalist in order to get the stories. And I'm kind of scared to talk to people a lot of the time. What this journalist needs to figure out is how do I go about getting all the skills and abilities of a real superhero?

WEDNESDAY, SEPTEMBER 10

Today Ms. King said that in addition to her grading the Superhero Slam projects, we will also have a bonus mark component. The bonus marks will come from how well we can include work from our other classes — she specifically pointed out Science — in our Superhero Slam.

My heart soared at the thought of getting bonus marks for reading comics! And being able to work on this project across a bunch of different classes. Then my heart plummeted when Ms. King made a very startling announcement . . . I was surprised and by the looks of my classmates, they were too. But in hindsight we shouldn't have been because the name says it all: a "slam" is a competition. All of us were too excited about choosing superheroes to think about the competition part. But just like in every comic, there has to be a challenge, and this one's mondo. We will have a debating tournament that pits each of our superheroes against each other!

A debating tournament means talking in front of everyone — the whole class!

Great!? My excitement is definitely down a notch. I am not a big fan of talking or presenting in front of people. Maybe I can be an invisible superhero and talk from outside the room.

Ms. King said she wants us to really think about making a difference in the world. She wants us to use superheroes because she calls them "modern-day mythologies of heroes."

In the written part of our Superhero Slam projects, Ms. King told us we are supposed to:

* Define what a hero is and why our society created superheroes.
* Choose a superhero and explain the super-powers that define that hero.
* Explain why we'd like to be that superhero or have those powers.
* Decide what we would do to make the world a better place using that power. Would it be all good? Is there a downside to being a superhero?

I wrote down exactly what Ms. King said about the project so I could include it here: "Since we're using a tournament format, your grade on the Superhero

Slam will be based on how well you do in debates against your classmates. For each round of the competition you will have two minutes to explain why your superhero is great and how she or he can help the world. You will each then have one more minute to explain how your superhero beats the other superhero on one of eight superhero categories. You will have to do a lot of research and thinking because you will randomly draw a card with one of the categories on it. You must always expect the unexpected!"

Here are the categories, or, as I like to call them "The Superhero Slam Great 8":

* Wisdom and experience
* Physical strength and agility
* Perseverance and determination
* Critical thinking
* Recovery
* Courage
* Preparation
* Leadership

My head was swirling from all this. Can we say "project made for Jessie"? That wasn't the only exciting news of the day. Ms. King got everyone's attention when she said, "To help kick off our projects on heroes, a friend of mine is coming by on Thursday when we'll be talking about September 11, 2001. Mike is a retired sergeant in the New York City Police Department. He was at Ground Zero that day when the Twin Towers fell in Manhattan. He has quite a story to tell us about his life and experiences. He is going to help provide some 'inspiration for the perspiration' you will put into your projects!"

Ms. King explained that those September 11 attacks were a series of four coordinated terrorist attacks. The terrorists hijacked the planes and then used them as bombs to fly into buildings. Two of the jets crashed into the World Trade Center in New York City, one was going to the White House in Washington but crashed on the way, and one slammed into the Pentagon in Washington. Very scary.

To meet someone who was really at such an event (and did something to help) will be really amazing.

While I was thinking about what it will be like to meet this police guy (one thing it means is less homework that night because special guests always mean lots of talk and very little homework), I was sort of zoning out – and starting to obsess a little bit about the debate.

Suddenly I heard, "Jessie, is there a hero in there somewhere?" Ms. King was, of course, standing right in front of my desk and looking down at me. She definitely looked friendly, but still it freaked me out. I did that jerky-yikes thing you do when somebody sort of sneaks up on you and you had no idea they were there.

Or like when I fall asleep sometimes. Maybe I was dozing off, but not on purpose. This back-to-school thing means getting up REALLY EARLY again. And it's messing with my schedule. Where is the 10 a.m. start time I requested?

Ms. King smiled at me and continued, "Do you think you have what it takes? Do you think you know what a hero is?"

Now, in case it isn't clear already from the daydreaming and the not-putting-up-my-hand, I don't like to talk much in class. I'm pretty shy in bigger groups. So the best I managed when I regained my senses was to stammer out an "Er, um." Of course, later, like NOW when it doesn't help, I have an answer: "What is a real hero anyway? How should I know? I'm in grade 8!"

But I didn't say that in class and managed only to quickly add, "Uh . . . heroes do . . . heroic things, I guess . . . err, when you need them to . . . do stuff?"

UGH! SO. EMBARRASSING.

But I guess heroes would be able to tackle heavy questions, even with sleepy brains. We're having an assembly this week all about heroes and heroic actions on 9/11 and after. It got us all thinking. And it got me thinking more and more about superheroes.

Cade — my best guy friend — is really excited by the whole idea of heroes. He likes to play the hero, and he's done some pretty heroic stuff on the basketball court and in the pool for our school teams. Along with Audrey — my best girl friend — the three of us generally hang out together after class and sit near each other in class.

Or try to.

We often get separated so we don't get too goofy. It's not like we're troublemakers like Dylan — my NOT best guy friend — we just make each other laugh and giggle a lot.

Actually Cade and Audrey do and say most of the stuff that's funny and I do most of the giggling. But we all wind up viewing the class from different seats.

Which might not be such a bad thing this year. Superhero Slam sounds awesome, but it's also going to be a lot of work.

Good thing a lot of that work will include reading comic books and thinking about superheroes!

THURSDAY, SEPTEMBER 11

It's been a long time since September 11, 2001, but all the news coverage still seems so creepy. Lots of images on TV and online today about 9/11. Pretty freaky. And we had that special visitor friend of Ms. King.

This guy was an incredible speaker. His name is Mike Bruen and he was a sergeant — he's retired now — in the New York City Police Department.

So he was pretty important and saw a lot of crazy stuff. Wow, the stuff he saw and did. He was, like, right there at Ground Zero. Lots of dust and smoke made it hard to see and to breathe even.

Ms. King asked Mike a bunch of questions, so we could learn about his experiences. He was so amazing that I wrote a lot of what he said down even though we didn't have to take notes.

Ms. King: "Did 9/11 seem real to you when it was happening? You were actually there. But every time we all look at videos and TV shows about it each year, it just seems like we're watching a movie or something that's just not real."

Mike Bruen: "That's some question ... did 9/11 seem real to me? Well, let me tell you kids, it was so real – it was overwhelming. You looked up and around at places that you have seen a million times and they were just ... gone.

"People around me were walking around in shock. At times like these, you have to be careful to not take in too much. I forgot all about tomorrow or next week and just thought about now. And how I was going to deal with the next few minutes or how I could take the next few steps.

"I tried to make each step a focused step because, the truth is, I realized they could be my last. Sorry! I've gotten pretty serious here – but you did ask, right?

"I tried to think for the people who couldn't. Because they were in shock and scared. That kind of thing is something I saw a lot in my career as a police officer. It gets easier to do with practice.

"People who depend on you kind of feed your ability to take charge. And the cool thing is they somehow become more confident because of your confidence.

"So I just focused on the tasks at hand — the little things, the little steps that I saw in front of me. That's how I did it.

"Occasionally, me and my friends, when time allowed, we lifted our heads to look at the big picture. And it was unbelievable. You cannot understand the level of destruction.

"About a week or so later, my group of detectives in the NYPD left the hole (or kind of a pile) that used to be the World Trade Center and spent 12 hours at the Staten Island dump sifting through wreckage and remains.

"We did a hundred-yard field at a time. Standing shoulder to shoulder with other officers, looking for something we could recognize as anything but pulverized rubble.

"After a few passes, we found nothing. So I got my line together and said, 'The first person who finds anything recognizable of any life being present, bring it to me.'

"About six hours later, the line was stopped by a detective. As he came towards me, he held up a green and white highlighter pen. This image remains seared into my memory. This was the first thing that showed us we weren't on the barren landscape of another planet. This was the only thing remotely human we found.

"That is devastation."

Before he came into our class, Ms. King had showed us a couple of news videos and summaries of what happened. Almost 3,000 people died in this tragedy. It is hard to even understand what that number means.

And to hear from somebody who was actually there and trying to help everyone was pretty mind-blowing. Mike said it was total mayhem with dust everywhere and people going every which way. The police and fire service people weren't just going every which way. They were all going to the World Trade Center.

And at the World Trade Center, everything was out of control. The police were rushing all around trying to help whoever needed help. Which was basically everyone.

Today I learned something important about heroes from Sergeant Mike Bruen.

Real heroes run towards — not away from — danger.

MONDAY, SEPTEMBER 15

Today in Science we had a mongo, uber convo about how we could get extra credit this year by working science into our Superhero Slam projects. Audrey got so excited she was almost bursting. But I was having a bit of trouble processing this.

I was still overwhelmed by thoughts of a year-long project! It's starting to sink in. When I got my science brain thinking again, Mr. Richardson was asking us to consider nature and nurture.

Mr. Richardson: "Are we born or made?" Which made me think about Socials and Ms. King asking the same thing about heroes. I think my teachers are all obsessing a bit too much on the same question! But on the upside, maybe that means I only have to think about one answer!

"What do you think, Cade?" Mr. Richardson asked while floating over to my pal on the other side of the class. Cade, after an initial blank look, said, "Um. Both maybe? Do I have to pick one?"

Mr. Richardson started laughing so hard and got very excited. We all thought he was going to pass right out in class. I think he may have hopped around a little bit even.

"That's it! Exactly! That's the right approach. Do you have to pick one? It's the question science has been asking for many years now, for centuries actually . . ." And then he kind of went off on another tangent about the history of science.

Cade and I made faces at each other across the room. He pretended to dramatically wipe sweat off his forehead for giving Mr. Richardson a good answer, so I shot him a quick thumbs-up.

Cade's pretty cool. He likes comics and science. And he's pretty sporty. He likes water wet as a swimmer and frozen as a snowboarder. He's also a great basketball player. He is always carrying a basketball around with him. But then so is Dylan, so let's not dwell too much on that.

Cade and I have been friends forever. Dylan and I, pretty much the opposite. But again, let's not dwell.

Back to the big questions. Mr. Richardson seemed to be saying the questions raised more questions. Huh? I guess we are supposed to have more answers by the end of the school year.

While Cade and I were having our moment, I saw Audrey busy scribbling away in her notebook. Scribbling like crazy. She was working so fast and so hard I thought the paper was going to burst into flames! In fact, I think I saw flames coming out of the bottom of a sketch Audrey was working on. The bit I saw looked like a robot or something. She looked up, gave me a little grin and eyebrow raise, and closed her notebook.

Anyway, all that talk of nature (me being born as me), nurture (me being shaped into me), and then heroes (could I be one?) had me all jazzed up when the bell went off.

24

Me: "Hey Audrey! How about the — "

Audrey: "Superhero Slam? I know, right? I never thought we'd get such a cool project in Socials! And we can use SCIENCE TOO!"

Me: "Uh, yeah. That's what I was going to say."

Cade: "Can't wait to get home and tell my brother — again! — to keep his hands off my comic book collection! But now I have a real school project to enforce the rule. I'm going to need them all for my research."

He finished off with a high five with Audrey. I tried to join in but he didn't see me holding up my hand, so I turned it into a kind of awkward wave.

As I drifted off for the next class and Cade and Audrey went off to swim practice (she joined the team this year), a big question hit me — KAPOW! Do I have any little bit of hero inside of me? How can I figure that out?

WEDNESDAY, SEPTEMBER 17

Dylan. Is. Such. A. Pain. I know I just need to ignore him, but sometimes it's SO HARD. Like today when Cade, Audrey, and me were all talking about the Superhero Slam. Dylan wandered by, listened in for a bit, and then told me I could never be a real superhero. Say what?? He said I was definitely in the "sidekick category" and then walked away. This made me very mad, which I showed to the whole world by . . . not saying anything

25

at all. Audrey moved to go after him but I pulled her back. I told them to just ignore Dylan.

But then I thought about it. What would it really be like to be a superhero?

Everyone plays dress-up these days — Halloween, comic book conventions, whatever. People like to pretend to be superheroes. But I can't get Mike Bruen's visit out of my head. He was talking about REAL HEROES. And superheroes are heroes with some added powers and stuff. Ms. King had me thinking, Could I be a hero? I could use the Superhero Slam to see what it takes to be a superhero, and then see if I have what it takes to be a hero — a superhero minus the superpower.

And then I'll show Dylan I'm no sidekick!

It would be a lot of work, but my dad always says if it is worth doing, it is worth doing well. Sometimes dads ARE actually right. Yep. SOME of the time dads are right. But each and every time they are, it's annoying. I might as well go all the way with this mission — let's call it Project Superhero — and really feel what it would be like to be a superhero. I mean, there probably won't be any fighting of supervillains (at least I hope not!), but maybe I can learn to run faster, speak up more, and kick butt.

And if I wind up with a fantastic mark on the Superhero Slam AND prove to Dylan that he's wrong about me, how good will that feel?!

THURSDAY, SEPTEMBER 18

I like pretty much all comic book superheroes, but my favorites are the ones I can relate to, like Batman or Iron Man. They are just people. People with lots of technology and loads of training, but still people.

Don't get me wrong, Superman is good (I ALMOST wrote "super"). Wolverine is wild. I like the X-Men. Storm is smashing, and Rogue rocks. Invisible Girl has some great powers. Like — she's invisible! That would be so handy at school! I can seriously relate to wanting to have some AMAZING powers.

But I can't actually relate to some superheroes because I can't experience things the way they do, no matter what. I can't be born on Krypton like Superman or have an adamantium skeleton like Wolverine. (Even Wikipedia says adamantium doesn't exist. Yet.) Or control the weather like Storm. Or be invisible like Invisible Girl. But being human, I can do that!

But which super-human superhero is right for me? Which one should the "New Jessie" try to be? I think comic books hold the answer. Archie, step aside. Betty and Veronica, talk to the hand. I need some heavy hitters.

So here's my strategy — Jessie's Plan of . . . Superhero Project Planning. (Note: I need a better title for this.)

> * Look through comics for inspiration and figure out who my role model will be.
> * Find out what it would take to get from here (Jessie) to there (Super-Jessie).

          * Rock my project and maybe try out some
            training myself . . .

The only problem with this plan is . . . can I really do
the last bit? I mean, CAN I do it? I'm not the most
"physically gifted" girl in school, I will be the first to
admit. I'm not super-charged and I don't pick up on how
to do things very quickly. Also, I'm Miss Uncompetitive.

Is this a challenge I can handle?

FRIDAY, SEPTEMBER 19

Checked in with some of my friends today. I wanted to
know what they are coming up with for the Superhero
Slam. We're still trying to decide what superheroes
we'll be for the tournament. A few of them (Kayli and
Amanda) are in band with me. I played the flute and

then the cello, and then since I wasn't really all that great I played . . . nothing. Kayli and I also did ballet together for a while. Well, she did ballet, I did my awkward version of little dance movements that hoped to be ballet when they got bigger and grew up. Amanda

is a former gymnastics buddy. Again, she did gymnastics, I did some jumping and rolling but I wasn't especially good at it. There's a theme here.

And as I mentioned before, there's my best friend, Audrey, who also swaps comics back and forth with me. She's been my friend for, like, nine years. We met in pre-school when we were both four. Well, I guess when one of us (NOT ME!) was four. The other (ME!) was five. My birthday is four months before Audrey's, so I'm OLDER. And wiser. About the ways of the world. Sometimes. At least between the two of us. I don't show it much around others.

Sometimes Audrey forgets to return my comics . . .
She loves them almost as much as I do – especially
the team-up comics like JUSTICE LEAGUE, BIRDS
OF PREY, and THE AVENGERS – so who's counting,
really?

OK. I am actually counting. I know she has four of my
JUSTICE LEAGUE and two of my FLASH comics . . . I
keep meaning to grab them from her room when I am
over at her place. But her room is just such a mess. If
I tried to grab those comics, I would have likely been
buried alive under an avalanche of Audrey's other gear!

Actually, it's not all Audrey's stuff. Most of the things
all over her room are electronics and computers. She
is so smart and good at doing things – and is so there
for her friends – that she's always fixing up stuff for
people for free. She's already repaired Cade's remote-
control submarine four times.

She even solved a computer problem for Mr.
Richardson last year.

But all that helping other people means being busy all
the time. And it means lots of stuff everywhere with
very little time (or interest) for cleaning up. Somehow
Audrey knows where everything is despite the mess
and despite what parents see when they look at a room
like that!

Seriously, I'd like Mom to swing by Audrey's room the
next time she gives my room the old inspection routine.
I admit my room doesn't always look awesome. But
Audrey's would be a real wake-up call for my mom!

But enough of that for now. Time for a snack . . . salad tastes better with dressing. My old pet guinea pig, Alfalfa, used to eat lettuce, carrots, and cucumbers too. But when we were feeding him, I am sure that the squeaky noises and twitching whiskers were crying out "Dressing! Dressing! Some tasty dressing PLEASE!"

Or maybe he just wanted out of his cage.

I doubt animals think much about nutrition and how food is like fuel for the body. Which is something I've been thinking about lately.

Anyway, pets are great friends even if they think different thoughts from me! Just like my human friends. I don't think about technology and computers the same way that Audrey does. But we are still the best of buds. And anyway, being different means we learn from each other. Maybe I can try to be as good about analyzing things as she is.

I can start with this superhero project. I can tell I'll have a lot to analyze — a whole year's worth of information I haven't even learned yet!

MONDAY, SEPTEMBER 22

I'm pretty steamed! I am not sure if teenaged boys are even human?! OK. OK. Mr. Richardson did teach us about the ways scientists organize life. The old domain, kingdom, phylum, class, order, family, genus, and species thing. So, according to science, Dylan is (likely) in the same species as me (human). But wow, according to my own experience, he must be a distant "caveman" relation.

I have had my fill of Dylan and his evil ways. After gym class, Audrey and Dylan were arguing about whether women or men are better athletes. I don't remember how or why that crazy conversation even got started, but it got pretty intense. I think Audrey was still mad at him for what he said to me last week, and that didn't help things.

They were acting like three-year-old kids, not grade 8s. And somehow the argument jumped into a fictional battle of men against women.

To summarize, here's what they agreed on:

> * Men and women are awesome. (Truth: they didn't exactly agree, not technically. Audrey said women were awesome, Dylan said men were awesome. So they agreed that someone was awesome, they just didn't agree that the other one was awesome too!)
> * Professional athletes (men or women) would both beat either of them. (Truth: they did agree about this.)

Here's what they disagreed about:

> * Everything else.

Anyway, their little chat rapidly became one big men versus women, no holds barred shouting match. It was as bad as "my dad can beat your dad." Actually more like, "My mom can beat your dad." Ha!

Dylan just said, "Men are better. At everything. So there."

"Wow, dude, nice argument. Logic much?" was Audrey's fantastic retort.

Just then, Ms. King piped up. Apparently she had been around the corner and had finally had enough of the witty exchange between Dylan and Audrey.

"Ever heard of the tennis players Billie Jean King and Bobby Riggs?" she asked, in that way teachers do when they know for sure you don't know what they are talking about. But they ask it anyway just to give you a chance. Or to make it seem like you have so much to learn . . . or maybe just so they can feel smarter!

> Audrey: "Huh?"

> Dylan: "Who?"

> Me: "Errr . . ."

Blank faces all around. Dylan and Audrey just looked at each other — who are Billie Jean King and Bobby Riggs? Finally, common ground — neither had any clue on this one.

"Billie Jean King was a famous women's tennis champion who played from 1959 to 1990," Ms. King informed us. "And, I know what you are thinking, but even though we have the same last name we aren't related. Too bad! I would so love to meet her.

"She won almost 700 matches and lost only about 150 times. She was the real deal." That was Ms. King getting all hip and with it. And not doing too bad a job of it, really.

"While Billie Jean was winning all her matches, an older gentleman named Bobby Riggs came along and started saying bad things about female tennis players. Basically he said he could beat any woman tennis player anytime, anywhere."

By this point Ms. King was on a bit of a roll — she seems to do this a lot. So naturally we got another question.

"Can you guess what Billie Jean did about that?"

"Well, I'd guess . . ." I surprised myself by getting involved and speaking up, but I wasn't surprised that I got interrupted.

"She got destroyed by Bobby Riggs!" Dylan shouted over my hesitant beginning.

Apparently Billie Jean took Bobby up on his boast on a TV show called BATTLE OF THE SEXES. Kind of like reality TV but from back in the day. When TV was really real. (So says Mom.)

"In full view of TV cameras and millions of viewers, they played a best of five set match to see about men versus women. Guess what happened?" Ms. King, again with the leading question. Although this time I think she thought we might actually know the answer. Or at least I might.

So Audrey jumped in quickly. "I figure she beat Mr. Mouthy!"

"Bobby Riggs," Ms. King said, smiling at Dylan, "lost each and every match."

Dylan, who already didn't look pleased, looked even worse when Audrey leaned in close and added two words: "EPIC," and Audrey left a very dramatic pause before a clear "FAIL."

Ms. King went down the hall, practically skipping after her fabulous teaching moment.

Unfortunately for clear thinkers everywhere, Dylan didn't get the message and he and Audrey continued to argue.

Arguing with Dylan is just too tempting, it has to be said. The number of ridiculous things that boy can spew out in a single sentence is amazing. If only we could change his powers for evil into powers for good.

At one point I shouted something about how Batgirl could so take down Batman.

Anyway, Dylan didn't even look at me and just carried on yelling at Audrey.

> Dylan: "Batman taught Batgirl, you know."
>
> Audrey: "Yes, Dylan, I know that. So does anyone who ever read Batman or Batgirl comics."
>
> Dylan: "Well, Batgirl couldn't even take out Batman Junior — Robin. Which is a lame bird anyway."

Audrey: "Hey Dylan, easy on the witty comments. Why would I even care if Batgirl could beat Batman? Why would she go around trying to beat her teacher anyway? Doesn't make sense. And Robin was taught by Batman too. So they wouldn't fight each other either."

Dylan: "Well . . . comics aren't for girls anyway."

Me: "?"

Audrey (getting very angry): "?!?!?!"

Dylan (seizing the moment): "Yeah. Comics are for boys. And most of the writers and artists are all guys. So there."

Me: "Err . . ."

I didn't have much to say actually, and neither did Audrey. He kind of got us there. Not that comics are for guys — only a jerk would actually say or believe that. But he was right that a lot of comic book people have been guys.

The thing is, there really aren't that many women or girl superheroes. Or are there?

I clearly needed to do some more research! It was time to visit my second favorite place in the world (besides my awesome bedroom) — Curious Comics.

TUESDAY, SEPTEMBER 23

This I know for sure — my superhero is going to be
female so I can beat Dylan. And rub it in. But which girl
superhero? I figured a good place to do some research
was at Curious Comics, my go-to shop for everything
comics related, with my comic book queen, Ricki.

Ricki knows EVERYTHING, and she is always super helpful. She works part-time at Curious Comics. When she was younger she went to my same middle school. But now she's 19 and taking Fine Arts (she is completely AWESOME) at the college. I never feel shy or awkward talking to Ricki.

Bat-tacular Comic Book Trivia — courtesy of Ricki: She asked me who the first female comic book superhero was. I knew she was probably expecting me to say Wonder Woman, and I did say that. But that's not who it was. It was . . . wait for it — The Red Tornado! The Red Tornado appeared in November 1940 in ALL-AMERICAN COMICS #20.

Before I got a chance to see Red Tornado, just the name alone immediately brought these fantastic thoughts into my head:

> * Sounds like a cool name. Red is a kicking color and tornadoes are powerful!
> * Sounds like an inspirational first-ever female comic book superhero!
> * Sounds like it might be too good to be true!

Yes, before I got a chance to see Red Tornado, it SOUNDED like all kinds of good. Then I learned that Red was originally Abigail Mathilda Hunkel who debuted in the same comic title (but issue #3) in June 1939. She was pretty mobile and moved pretty quickly and powerfully — thus the Tornado name — but her costume was kind of lame.

Her costume was basically a long underwear onesie.

Red, of course, not that the name "Red Tornado" was a giveaway or anything.

The best of the worst (or the least worst of the worst?) was . . . I am actually having a hard time writing this without giggling. OK. Phew. I stopped. Big breath. Better.

The worst part was that she wore a cooking pot on her head. AS A HELMET. The cooking pot had eyeholes, of course. So that modification for sure made it better. (Sarcasm.)

I can imagine the bad dudes talking among themselves. "Hey, that superhero has a cooking pot on her head. Easy peasy. I think we can do whatever criminal thing we want now."

But then they really look at the cooking pot and say, "Wait a minute, there are eyeholes in the pot! We had better be careful after all, she seems to have the power of sight."

Great.

And her preferred nickname was "Ma." Doesn't exactly strike fear into the hearts of criminals (unless you're afraid of your mother?). But, despite the downside of that bit of comic-book history, there are actually some pretty powerful women superheroes. Wonder Woman, Invisible Girl from Fantastic Four, Storm and Rogue from X-Men.

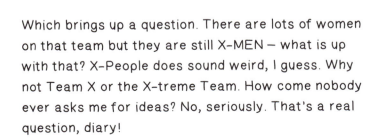

Which brings up a question. There are lots of women on that team but they are still X-MEN — what is up with that? X-People does sound weird, I guess. Why not Team X or the X-treme Team. How come nobody ever asks me for ideas? No, seriously. That's a real question, diary!

Then there's Black Canary from Birds of Prey (very cool name), Elektra, Power Girl, and Huntress. Ricki also mentioned Zatanna. Who has cool sorcery powers, but I am kind of not so much into "magical intervention" when it comes to superheroes. So Zatanna is definitely out for my project.

After looking over all the contenders, surfing the web for random (and often finding really weird) commentary and fan factoids, and then bouncing some ideas off Ricki, I came up with my top 6.

I was originally shooting for a top 5 but failed. Since this is my list though, I can have six if I want. ~~The Spectacular Six . . .~~ No! The SUPER SIX . . .

Number 6: Wonder Woman
She is mega-powerful and Ricki says Wonder Woman is only just slightly behind Superman in strength. She is a good fighter — Wonder Woman is a "Warrior Princess of the Amazon" after all — and can take a lot of fighting action without getting injured. It would be way cool to be Wonder Woman. EXCEPT she was born in a fictional Amazonian place called Paradise Island. Which is a bizarre reason to have superpowers, actually. Also, she has a WAY over the top outfit. Or under the top actually. Or a very sketchy top on top. My dad would so not approve. The boots are okay, but the shorts and top need work. As in, doing some work to get rid of them. Completely. ☹ Seriously, who goes to a fight wearing a bathing suit? OK. Aquaman does. And so does Namor the Sub-Mariner. But they literally live in the ocean, so that makes sense. My main reason

for saying no to Wonder Woman comes down to her powers basically being magical. In comics, I like it when the superheroes have to use their wits and skills to get out of trouble instead of just waving their wands (or magic lasso).

Number 5: Invisible Girl from Fantastic Four
Very cool. She can be, well, invisible. And put forcefields around stuff. Which is pretty neat. She got her powers from a big jolt of "cosmic radiation" while on a space mission. Well, the cosmic radiation thing doesn't make sense . . . Shouldn't all stewardesses have superpowers then? And every astronaut ever? Too bad. She has a rocking blue jumpsuit that I quite like!

Number 4: Storm from X-Men (I won't go off on the problem with this team name again)
Very clever and tricky, Storm can control the weather. Why can she control the weather? Instead of a reason I can work with, well, this is where it all goes sadly wrong. Storm can control the weather because she was born in Africa and got some African sorceress powers along with her cleverness and stylish fashion sense. SIGH. Storm comes down to sorcery and magic like Wonder Woman. Plus, no matter how upset I have been in my life (and it must be mentioned that Mom has asked me to turn down the drama on occasion . . . OK, perhaps on a few occasions), I have never created any actual tornadoes. Not even despite my best (worst?) efforts a small hailstorm. And I certainly can't TURN OFF the rain we get here during our Pacific Northwest fall.

Number 3: Black Canary from Birds of Prey
Unlike X-Men, I like the name Birds of Prey. A lot.
Canary's an awesome fighter. She also has a
supersonic scream that can knock things down. As in
flatten them like a shockwave from a bomb going off
does. She got her scream from radiation or something
back in the 1940s. They really had a thing for radiation
in those days. Good thing they didn't have microwave
ovens back then. Everybody would be some kind of
radiation superhero. Sadly I have to admit that the
supersonic scream thing is a bit silly. I mean, even
if she could have that scream, how come her head
doesn't explode? OK. OK. Yes, yes, yes, I know it's
a comic book. Fiction. But I notice this stuff! And I
just looked it up in the GUINNESS BOOK OF WORLD
RECORDS: in 2000 Jill Drake had the loudest scream
recorded at 129 decibels. That's almost as loud as a
jet engine! But not loud enough to knock anybody over.
Ugh. Four down and only two left to go. The field is
narrowing.

Number 2: Elektra

Elektra really looked promising. She is a mega-skilled martial artist just like my Auntie G! And she has a cool red outfit. Elektra does, I mean, not my Auntie! AND she began training while she was barely a teen. She'd be a good female superhero role model to think about. If we stopped right here. But . . . Ding. Ding. Ding. Uh oh, are those alarm bells? Unfortunately, Elektra has this really bad habit of killing people. A lot of people. A ridiculously large number of people. And she kills them often. (Not the same people, of course, different people each time.) Elektra is basically an assassin. A very, very good assassin. And that isn't Auntie G approved (thankfully). And that isn't what I am looking for (also thankfully). So I am down to one more on my short list.

Number 1: Batgirl

Batgirl's an awesome fighter. She is super well trained in acrobatics, gymnastics, and martial arts. She also got lots of training tips from Batman. Talk about training with the best! As part of the Bat-Family, Batgirl also has the same ethical code as Batman. No killing! She is also way smart. Ricki says in some versions Batgirl even has a doctorate – just like Mom! She is the most realistic superhero worth trying to be that I am likely to find. So, Batgirl it is. ☺

This could get intense. Being my detail-oriented self, I'll start with what I know. Also, my inner journalist-in-training always has lots of questions that need asking. Or, I should say, my inner journalist always wants answers to questions I ask!

My dad's the one who always says that I'm a little bit detail-oriented. He says he's glad I "can see the forest and the trees," but sometimes I do wind up "chewing on the bark." Eww, Dad, really? My dad needs to get outside LESS.

But he actually may have a point there. I'm pretty sure my grade 5 class presentation on ALICE IN WONDERLAND wasn't necessarily helped by the 15 minutes I spent outlining the kinds of trees she would have come across. But I NEEDED TO KNOW, and I thought my classmates did too.

I'm curious. I need to know stuff. I ask questions. (Can we say scientist?) I get answers. (Can we say journalist?) It's who I am. (Can we say cool cat?) It's my style.

So there.

Now to think about all things Batgirl! I have so many questions. As Alice would say, I'm "curiouser and curiouser."

TUESDAY, SEPTEMBER 30

For the whole time I've known her, Audrey has always liked building and making inventions and gizmos. What used to be wooden blocks in pre-school have now become ultra-funky engineering circuits. For Audrey, what's truly amazing is what you can do with technology, and what she can do is make some crazy robots.

Audrey has made some major stuff with her circuits! You can program her little robots to do all sorts of amazing things. She made a kind of plate-holder-with-wheels robot that would take her empty snack plate and cup from her room all the way to the kitchen.

Of course, she still had to go into the kitchen and put the plate and cup into the dishwasher. But — and this is pretty important — she did it LATER. When she felt like it. So there.

If only we could harness Audrey's powers for the true forces of good! Like putting MY dishes away. Or my laundry. Or both actually . . . and maybe it could do some of my math homework for me. Come here, little robot, come on now, I've got some algebra for you. It won't hurt you at all . . .

Anyway, I let Audrey in on my plan today.

Me: "So, I am going to be a girl superhero. And

then I'm going to beat Dylan. I'm going to actually try and do some of the training myself. It will be awesome!"

Audrey: "OK. Cool! But don't you think this is getting a little personal already? It's just Dylan after all."

Me: "No, after that Billie Jean King throwdown, he's got this coming. And maybe it is personal. Dylan's superpower is clearly to annoy me. He's like some kind of annoying kryptonite to my supergirl-ness."

Audrey: "I don't know why you're making more work for yourself. We already have so many projects!"

Me (kind of mumbling and trailing off): ". . . the training and research will help me prepare for the Slam."

Audrey: "I've decided I'm going with a superhero I could make."

Me: "Um, please tell me you don't mean 'make' as in Frankenstein or some other kind of zombie apocalypse reject?"

Audrey: "Interesting, but no. 'Make' as in make a robot suit of armor. 'Make,' like, as in robots and machines — did I hear someone say Iron Man? Or maybe Iron Woman? But instead of an Iron Man suit for fighting the good fight, mine will be for helping people. For my bonus marks in Science,

I'm going to sketch out plans for a real armored exoskeleton."

She then went on to describe her exoskeleton design as a kind of "power pack for people" (her lingo). I think this is probably what happens when your mom is an engineer.

Her "people power pack" or "the big P3" (my lingo) idea is actually pretty amazing. Audrey got the idea when we were watching a TV show where a guy got robot legs to help him walk. Audrey looked it up and you can actually buy those legs. If you have enough money.

It is way expensive. Like $100,000. Which is apparently quite an awful lot of money. I just worked out that I could buy almost 35,000 comics with that amount of cash. I could just sit and read in my room forever!

The thing is, Audrey wants to help people. She's considerate and compassionate like that. She thinks she can make robot legs a lot cheaper and then more people could use them.

Despite her being awesome though, we don't completely agree here on this issue of making a superhero.

I think training and enhancing your innate abilities is the way to go. Hello, Batgirl. Audrey argued that the only way to true superhero-ness (or superhero-dom, or superhero-ocity; we couldn't decide which word is correct) was through technology. "Technology triumphs over training," she said.

Audrey even said she'd prove it to me one day. She dreams of building a full-on Iron Man exoskeleton to help people who can't move very well. While I am totally in favor of helping people, I think it's more important to be able to help yourself. By doing push-ups.

So the Jessie-Audrey Superhero Battle Royale is on. Winner gets bragging rights and the loser . . . well, we didn't really come up with anything opposite for that. So I guess the loser gets not bragging rights. We will have to come up with something to spice this up.

We'll see who (me) is right in June! I'm not even a superhero yet and already I've got so many battles to fight! Bring it on.

But before then, I've got a lot of work ahead of me. I need a real plan here for some first-hand Batgirl training!

WEDNESDAY, OCTOBER 8

* Preparation *   My little exploration of the real
                   life of Batgirl means my list of
                   superhero skills and abilities
includes some very specific physical training.

To experience real Batgirl training, I need to learn:

    * Martial arts
        - Punching and kicking
        - Throwing
        - Using martial arts weapons, like sticks
        - Falling (and
          getting up)
    * Running
    * Jumping
    * Gymnastics
        - Acrobatics
        - Leaping

        - Climbing
    * Detective stuff

Looking over my list, falling seems quite important.

Actually, getting up again seems the most important bit. The good news is, I sure have loads of experience in falling (and getting right back up) from all those hours of

figure skating! Of course, I was only falling by myself after another failed attempt at an axel, not being thrown by somebody. But those are just details, really, right?

Batgirl also tends to rip around on a motorcycle. Technically that should be on the list too. But I am going to pass on that seeing as how I don't have a driver's license. Or a motorcycle. Yet.

The Bat-Family is also super smart. And they almost always use brains instead of fighting. So Mom would definitely approve of anything that involves using brains over fists! To figure out my plan, I still need more info. That means reading some more comic books, surfing the internet a bit, and chatting with Ricki.

Dad says Auntie G has been doing karate since "Santa Claus was a young boy." Which is supposed to mean a long time, I guess. I wish Dad would just come right out and say exactly what he means sometimes!

Anyway, she was doing karate (empty hand fighting) and kobujutsu (fighting with weapons) way before she even had an email address! Back in the time of the dinosaurs. She loved it when I told her that. Not really, she didn't. But I'm her favorite (OK, oldest) niece so I can get away with some things. I admitted she was way younger than 65 million years old, back when the dinosaurs all died out!

Funny story about Auntie G and that email thing. Back when I was 10, I was begging all the time for an email address. I wanted one and wanted it now. This went on for weeks and months.

It came up again one day Auntie G was over. She's a graphic artist and got me into sketching and art. We share a lot of interests and she is usually on my side for things. She's an auntie, after all! So I shouted, "I should get an email address at the same age as Auntie G did!"

Immediately Mom and Dad said "OK, sounds good." I should have realized something strange was going on, but I plunged on. I was expecting something like her getting an email address at age nine or 10. Or even 11. Some reasonable age.

Nope! It turns out it was when she was 27! She is way OLD. Then they told me some stuff about how the internet wasn't even invented when she was a kid!

After that I didn't dare ask how old she was when she got her first cell phone . . . or how big it was. Too funny!

But it also really hit me that Auntie G has been training for SO LONG. Auntie G's got awesome skills from all those years of training. How far can I get in only a few months?

MONDAY, OCTOBER 20

Today I'm still feeling kind of sore from all the punching, kicking, and falling down practice I did with Auntie G on Saturday. She is very agile and a really good teacher. She is really tricky, actually, when she moves. When I tried to punch towards her, it was kind of like she disappeared and then reappeared ready to do something!

Then Sunday's rock climbing was very cool. Audrey is a total little monkey. They had a bell at the top of one of the climbing courses. You're supposed to ring it when you get up to the top. So there Audrey and I were, getting ready. You have to put on a safety harness and clip rope and a spotter runs the rope while you climb up the wall.

I finished all my clipping and tightening and I was right beside Audrey. Or so I thought. Somebody didn't wait for me.

> Me (looking at my own harness and thinking my friend was still there): "OK, Audie. Let's do it."
>
> Me (turning to look around where Audrey was supposed to be): "Audrey?"
>
> Sound from above: "Ding ding ding."

So I looked up and saw this crazy girl laughing her head off up at the top already. It was like something out of a cartoon. Audrey shot up the wall and rang the bell before I had even grabbed one of the "rocks" on the indoor climbing wall.

I am not sure if there is a "climbing gene," but if there is one, Audrey would explain the 95% genetic DNA overlap we have with chimpanzees.

It was really great that Audrey could meet up with me. I've been missing Audrey. She's been MIA lately. She was away from school last week and kind of off the grid. Her sister Melissa's been super tired lately and lots has been going on. She has had a bunch of blood tests and medical things done. Her whole family is really worried about her.

Audrey said today that they finally figured out Melissa has depression. Melissa's doing okay and Audrey's family is super supportive — they are all (almost) as cool as she is. It's been hard for everybody but they are getting through things.

Melissa's the best older sister. I sometimes wish she were mine. I can't imagine her not caring about anything. She's always so loud and fun.

I don't know if I could be as brave as Audrey.

WEDNESDAY, OCTOBER 22

Batgirl's spirit animal is obviously — and this isn't going to be a real surprise — a bat. Sure, they strike fear in the hearts of old ladies, but I gotta figure out why they're superhero-worthy.

Another trip up to the college put to good use! After school today, I met up with Mom at her lab. Before going by her building, I headed over to the nearby library to look into bats. They have a great section on pop culture.

I have spent a lot of time thinking about this fixation on bats that the Bat-Family has. It was all started by Bruce Wayne, of course, way back in DETECTIVE COMICS #27 in 1939. Actually, I learned at the library that it really all started with Bob Kane and Bill Finger who created "Bat-Man" together.

The famous comic-book line (from "The Batman Wars Against the Dirigible of Doom" DETECTIVE COMICS #33, November 1939) that everyone who writes comics is always using is that bad guys "are a superstitious and cowardly lot." In the original Bat-Man story, Bruce Wayne chose a bat because he wanted something that would scare the bad guys. But I don't find bats too scary, actually.

Anyway, after Ricki told me about this she asked if I had a copy of that 1939 comic book. Of course I said no! Then she told me that a copy in super good ("mint") condition sold a few years ago for more than $1 million! Yikes.

If I had a copy, even if it was in really poor condition, I would absolutely keep it.

But back to bats. I quite like bats as animals. They are kind of like furry mice with wings. Good ol' Kayli had two white mice as pets. She named them Zeke and Eek. Let's be honest: Kayli has kind of a limited imagination for names. They were cute, but a bit messy. OK. A lot messy. One did poo in my hand once. Seriously, it was gross.

In fact, last year, I saw this awesome PBS NOVA show on bats. The way bats can shriek and bounce sound around and use hearing and echolocation to "see" is cool. Kind of like dolphins. Except smaller. And dry. And furry. And they don't eat fish.

Or at least not whole fish all at once. But on the down side, bats do have toxic poo.

Yes.

Toxic.

Poo.

I couldn't believe that part. Bat poo has a special name even — guano. Which reminds me . . . I know all that poo is gone but I really have to go wash my hands. AGAIN.

The NOVA show said that a fungus can grow in the guano. And then it sprouts spores in the air and if you breathe them in, they can grow in your lungs! It was called "histoplasmosis." When I shared this with Mr. Richardson, he was very impressed.

So bats scare a lot of people for a lot of different reasons. Before I learned that, I thought a better choice for a superhero's spirit animal might have been something actually big and physically threatening. Like a silverback gorilla. Gorilla-Girl (or even Girl-Gorilla) has kind of a nice ring to it. And maybe a more powerful sound to it?

Plus we have a lot more in common with gorillas than with bats, don't we? Mr. Richardson told us that for a long time scientists thought gorillas were our closest relations among other animals. Now we know that it's actually chimpanzees who are closest to us genetically!

I'm sitting here scratching Coco's ear (and making her back leg do that funny thumping thing that dogs do — it's adorable). It's kind of funny, in a neat sort of way, to think that all animals are made up of the same stuff. I guess this is where last year's science class on

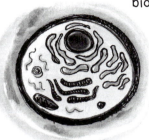

biology of the cell might come in handy. A bit of bat biology. Just what the doctor — Dr. Batgirl — ordered. Now, where're my notes from grade 7?

My takeaways from my bat research are:

* Bats are stealthy.
* Bats can fly.
* Bats have a kind of sonar called echolocation.
* Bats can communicate with each other.

If you take all those points and throw in the toxic poo, bats ARE kinda fearsome after all.

Just like genes that aren't working right and can change your body in bad ways, bats — and therefore Batgirl — can harm you without you knowing. They are stealthy and can communicate secretly and quietly and make trouble for bad guys. Watch out, Dylan!

OK. My little list of things I still gotta sort out (my need-to-knows):

* Exactly what kind of training do I have to look into? I need to make a plan of some kind here.
* How much time would it really take to become a superhero? I'm kinda suspecting more than a year!
* How important is having the genes for it? Jury is out on this so far!

Mr. Richardson said that "what's in our genes is in our jeans." He thought it was hilarious. But when we didn't laugh he had to write it on the board for us to get it. Most of us just heard "what's in our jeans is in our jeans." Which is kind of a weird thing to say. Poor Mr. Richardson. He really does try SO, SO hard.

FRIDAY, OCTOBER 24

* Perseverance * — Time to think about why and how Batgirl can be SO GOOD at so many different things. If I'm going to learn about this, I need to learn from the best. Since there aren't any actual real-life super-heroes I can talk to, I'm going with the next best thing — Olympic athletes! People are always saying athletes can do superhuman stuff, so I need to do some interviews to add to my training for Batgirl. Although it's kind of scary to interview people, it's good practice for my eventual career as a Pulitzer Prize—winning journalist. Of course, I'll just stick to interviewing them by letter. Talking to them in person or on the phone is way too scary to think about!

I remember watching speedskating at the Olympics one winter and Dad telling me that the red-haired athlete — Clara Hughes — also competed in the summer Olympics in cycling! Clara won four Olympic, six World Championship, and 13 World Cup medals for speed skating, and two Olympic, one World Championship, and three Commonwealth Games medals for cycling.

I couldn't imagine how hard she must train all the time!
So I wrote her a letter to find out.

Dear Clara,

My parents keep talking about how great you are
and all the stuff you have done in sports. They said
you are a great role model. You never know if your
parents are right about stuff like that, so I researched all about you. And then I wanted to write
and ask you about what it was like to be an Olym-
pian in both the winter and summer games.
    My Grade 8 project is about extreme human abil-
ities. I'm trying to figure out if a person could train
to become like the superhero Batgirl. Batgirl is really
good at lots of things, and since you are too it would
be great to ask you some questions! Also, Batgirl
had to overcome lots of difficulties in her life to get
so good at what she does. You are a great person to
ask about that too!
    For example, I read that you had depression,
and well, my best friend Audrey, her sister Melissa
(she's 16) has had lots of stuff going on the last
while. Her family just found out she has depression. So my questions have to do with persevering, I
guess.

Thanks for helping me with my project,
Jessie

Thanks for writing to me, Jessie! I am very happy to answer your questions.

How did you figure out that you had depression? And how do you get through it?

I was sleeping so much and never felt rested; I was crying so much not knowing why and unable to stop; I put on weight and felt like I was enveloped in darkness. I seriously didn't know anything was wrong with me and felt like I had to fix myself. It wasn't until a doctor talked to me about what she saw—that I was depressed—that I even considered it a possibility. I was able to get better through the help of others. Through counseling and changing my ideas as to how I needed to train and how much I could push myself as an athlete. Eventually I was able to have fun again in training for sport, but it took a long, long time. It was harder than anything I ever did in sport, getting through depression, and I could not do it alone.

It's pretty amazing that you did all the things you have done. Did your depression affect your training and competing?

I had to change my ideas of how much I could train and push myself. I also had to change my nutrition and pay better attention to the food I ate. I began to realize that not just in sport but in life as well that food is fuel and it directly affects my mood. Things like sugar, gluten, and dairy are not good for me. But I still love all those things so it takes a lot of discipline. I always remind myself the reward is feeling better!

What was harder, training to win an Olympic medal or talking so openly about your depression?

It was easy to be open about my experience with depression. What was so hard was being depressed. To be honest, I live with a low-grade fear of becoming depressed again, which only makes me make good choices each day for my state of mind. Training to win an Olympic medal was difficult, yes, but much of that was in my control. What I've figured out is that when I feel good, I can make sure I continue to do all the good steps—I guess, in ways the training—to maintain a good state of mental health. Both take discipline, that's for sure!

Did you find it difficult to train for speed skating and cycling? Did you do similar things for both?

The training in some ways was similar. I used the bike a lot for skating training. What I love most about cycling is that I did almost all my training outside in beautiful places. I skated indoors in circles and sometimes that was a bit monotonous. But the motion of skating is so beautiful . . . I still can't believe I was able to skate like that. It's like a dream.

When you were a kid how did you know you wanted to be an Olympic athlete?

I saw Gaétan Boucher skate in his last games and was hooked. Something inside me connected to the movement and I just knew, I felt it in my heart, that was what I was going to do in my life.

I have to know: do you have a favorite superhero?

I have a real live superhero and that is my mom. She is super-human to me!

Wow. Clara Hughes proves that a person can be not just good but great — an Olympic medalist — in more than one sport AND overcome difficulties. It's really cool that Clara was inspired by seeing someone else do something amazing, and now I'm inspired to do something myself because of Clara. Ms. King was right. Heroes, superheroes, and everyday people need (and can find) "inspiration for their perspiration."

But it still means you have to DO SOMETHING to get somewhere.

THURSDAY, OCTOBER 30

* Strength *

I've skipped ahead a little in our science textbook. Okay, way ahead. I do that sometimes. Lucky chapter 13 (it's a textbook so I'll write this using my formal voice): "Genetics and physical traits inherited from your parents."

So what do I have to work with, here?

* Me: Height 5-foot-4, weight 110 lbs, eye sight 20/20 (ish).
* Mom: Height 5-foot-8, weight 135 lbs, eye sight — seems good . . . so far. But she does lean in pretty close to the computer screen when she's working.
* Dad: Height 6-foot-2, weight 210 lbs, eye sight — meh. He wears glasses for "computer work."

My mom and dad are pretty active and in good shape. Me? Upper body strength? I can't even do a single chin-up on the monkey bars. When I picked Shay up from her school yesterday, I waited until the elementary kids cleared out with their parents and tried to do a few. At least no one was there to witness my humiliation.

Except Shay. Who did 10. Grr.

Lower body strength? Not bad. Got Shay to time my 100-meter dash. Time = 14 seconds. Not fantastic. Reflexes? Slow-ish. SIGH.

At least I can blame a bunch of it on my parents, according to Steiner and Young, the writers of WORLD OF BIOLOGY: A GRADE EIGHT PRIMER. I already knew that the body and brain change with practice and training.

But how much I can change my body has lots to do with that whole "genes in my jeans" thing. Mr. Richardson said our genes contain the blueprint for telling our cells — all 37 trillion of them — what to become and how to work.

So, what have my cells been told? (And how can I get them to listen better?) How do we know our "genetic potential"? This came up in another nature versus nurture debate we had in class. Mr. Richardson challenged everybody to find out some examples of genes and performance.

We did a "U-debate" to see what everyone thought about this and what we could all come up with. It was actually pretty good considering we only had one night to look up stuff. Lots of my classmates weren't too sure of their opinions and wanted to sit in the middle (at the bottom of the U) where you sit if you aren't so certain of your position.

Since the ends of the U are for extreme or very certain opinions, I usually sit in the middle if I can. I don't like to be controversial or flash my opinion too much, even when I do have one. But today sitting in the middle was actually correct.

Audrey told everyone that scientists have studied this kind of question by looking at the lives of identical twins. She read about some real twin athletes. And she was all set to tell us about them when Cade couldn't contain himself anymore and interrupted her!

Which turned out to be great because he interrupted with the most amazing thing! It was about this girl from the Ukraine that Cade learned about from a TV show he saw. She's named Varya Akulova. And she's really, really, strong, just like her mom, her dad, her dad's dad, his dad's dad's dad . . .

Holy crazy strong family, Batman.

How crazy strong? I couldn't believe what Cade told us, so I looked it up myself on Varya's own website. Here's a little list of what Varya could do when she was a kid:

* She could CARRY HER DAD on her back when she was six!
* At 14 she could lift four times her body weight! She weighed about 90 pounds, so that means she could lift over 350 pounds. Yikes.
* It isn't listed, but I bet she could do more than one chin-up and 13 push-ups. So she's likely got me beat there too . . .

Apparently her whole family is strong and they train and train all the time. Could I get THAT strong? How about just get stronger than I am? I told Mom all about this. Then she told me she ALREADY KNEW this story! She was at a conference last year on "genetics and exercise performance." They talked about a scientist guy named Dr. Schuelke – from a university in Berlin, Germany – who did a study on a different kid who was missing a certain gene. Mom said this is called "gene deletion." This kid's missing gene is called myostatin.

Normally myostatin keeps muscles from getting too big and too strong! Weird. So, it's my myostatin that is keeping me from becoming as strong and huge as the Incredible Hulk! (Or She-Hulk.) Apparently if you don't have myostatin, your muscles can get a lot stronger. At the conference, they talked about Varya but since nobody had done the gene test on her, they didn't know if she had the myostatin gene or not.

The thing Mom wanted me to "appreciate" (her word) is that you can have whatever genes you have (your nature). But if you don't do any training, nothing happens. The genes need to be turned on (she said "expressed") and your body needs to be trained (the nurture).

So you actually do need nurture to go along with nature.

How the body works seems so cool but so hard to understand at the same time. But it's all good stuff for my Superhero Slam project. I like to understand stuff and what I'm understanding is that training takes time and you can only do so much. But you don't know how much you can actually do until you try.

Time for a few more push-ups . . . and maybe some chin-ups . . . and sit-ups I guess. I'm not fantastic but I have potential!

MONDAY, NOVEMBER 10

* *
* Physical Strength *
          *

Well, I haven't had as many chances to hang out with Audrey and Cade as usual. It's not like they're ignoring me, it's just that they have a lot of extra swim team practices. Since they're both on the team and I am not (I'm not really a good swimmer, as it turns out), it's totally to be expected. But it still sucks and I miss seeing them outside class.

But at least I did some video chatting with Audrey today! I was so excited to tell her about Clara Hughes!

> Me: "I got an awesome answer back from Clara Hughes! She told me all about training for summer and winter Olympics, winning medals in both games, and that her mom's her superhero!"
>
> Audrey: "That is so cool! You are like celebrity grade 8 journalist girl!"
>
> Me (humbly): "Yeah! But even more interesting! Clara has depression too. But she got helped and worked through it like Melissa. And Clara has done awesome, just like Melissa will! Please tell her about that!"
>
> Audrey: "Oh for sure. I will. It's just like Cade told her at dinner last night. He was doing some reading about depression and how nowadays more people understand it and it's not something to be afraid of."
>
> Me (in my head): "Told her at dinner? What dinner? Did I miss an invite here? I guess since their parents take turns driving after practices they've stayed for dinner a few times.

Sounds like good hanging-out times. That I am missing. ☹ If only I were a better swimmer, I'd try for the team too!

Me (out loud in a normal and hopefully not hurt-sounding voice): "Yeah. Great. Cade. He's a great guy. Very supportive."

And then we kind of just said bye and hung up.

It kind of hurts being left out. Where have the three amigos gone? Maybe I couldn't make the swim team, but I am going to train so hard this year and prove to everyone that I can do physical stuff too!

THURSDAY, NOVEMBER 13

* Recovery *

Had a great moment with Ricki today. Nothing super cool comics-wise. But she did show me this new cool insulin pump she just got. Ricki's diabetic and has to give herself insulin injections. When I came into Curious Comics today, she said "Hey Jess! Guess who's part Iron Man now? I've got my own cyborg implant!"

She showed me this little package that was stuck on her arm. Inside was insulin and it gets injected into her blood by the implant whenever it's needed. There's a needle inside it that supplies insulin automatically. Amazing!

Now Ricki doesn't have to do her insulin injections all the time. It looks pretty futuristic. It really is a technological connection to the body and has an Iron Man vibe. I told her I'd bring Audrey by to check it out! (If I can find her . . .)

78

I remember Mr. Richardson telling us in science class that our bodies are, like, 60% water. About two-thirds of that water is in my cells and one-third kind of connects the cells together.

Some scientists from France, United States, and Canada spent a lot of time thinking about what this means for our bodies and how they work. They came up with a term called "homeostasis."

Mr. R. said homeostasis is basically balance in the body. And because of all that liquid, it turns out that floating hormones move all over the body to do practically everything.

Everything from my occasionally (OK, possibly often) shifting moods to how strong I can be. When homeostasis is not in balance because of a problem in the body, lots of things can go wrong. A big one that comes from problems with the pancreas, kidneys, and the level of sugar in the blood, is diabetes.

Mr. Richardson tried to gross us out by telling us that up until about 1100 CE people tested for diabetes by drinking urine to see if it was sweet! Y-U-C-K. I'm not sure if I'll tell Ricki about that one.

I am pretty sure she never checked out her pee like that. At least I hope not. Makes needles seem a lot more civilized anyway. And that new automatic pump seems like a real superhero invention.

Ricki's got the first kind, or type 1 juvenile diabetes. She found out when she was 12. She was always super tired and she was drinking lots and lots of water. And she said she was eating OK but kept losing weight. I know all this because I peppered her with questions! She lost 10 pounds one summer, she said. Her mom and dad were getting a bit worried that maybe she had diabetes or something. And they were right.

Part of how body balance works has to do with responding to stress. Stress is some kind of challenge to the body. Mr. Richardson said that a challenge to the body is met when the body responds to the stress by changing, so the effect of the stress is smaller. Err . . . we were all getting pretty confused at that point, so Mr. Richardson used the idea of playing a guitar.(I've always wanted to play guitar!)

When you first start to push on the strings, it hurts your fingers. That's the stress. Over time, you build up calluses on those fingers. Those calluses are thicker skin and are the body's response to reduce the stress of pushing on the strings. So it hurts less. But if you do too much too fast, you don't have time for a callus to form. So you get a blister.

Then Mr. Richardson went on with his "stress of life" talk (again). But this time about outer space! He is really into space travel and astronauts. I think Mr. Richardson wanted to be an astronaut himself, actually. But he is 6-foot-6 so he couldn't have been one anyway — he is over NASA's 6-foot-4 limit. Too bad, poor guy.

Today he combined some physics with some biology talking about the force of gravity and the cells in our bodies. The bottom line was that one of the reasons we actually have the form and shape we do is because the force of gravity from Earth is pulling on us all the time. And if you don't have that force, our bodies would really go downhill.

Well, Mr. Richardson said that's a big problem in space. Because there is no gravity, that stress isn't there and the body just gets flabby. It's going to be a big problem for traveling to other planets. Or even now, for astronauts on the Space Station.

Since I like to get first-hand information, I asked Mr. Richardson if I could write to some astronauts and ask them. It's a good bit of background research for understanding how human bodies change with stress. The stress on Batgirl in space! As soon as Mr. R. gets me an address, I'm going to write to somebody at NASA who's had a mission on the International Space Station.

Which reminds me of my main mission: what stresses do I need to have in order to help me become Batgirl? And how can it be done without becoming a blister?

* Recovery *

So I have a blister on my knuckles. This is pretty funny, considering how I finished my last entry. Auntie G was teaching me how to hit the punching bag. She told me to go slow and just do a little bit the first day. She told me I was training my skin and bones, not just my courage to hit something heavy (but kind of softish).

Yes. The heavy bag is soft but the covering likes to grab at your skin a bit. Auntie G said to do 50 punches with each hand and then stop. Enough for today. Let the skin thicken a bit and try again next time.

But I thought that more would be better, right? So, I did 200 with each hand.

I know, I know. After 100, my knuckles were getting red (and sore), but I pushed myself to do more. (I am going to show everyone!) I was determined to be tough! And then I was so tough, my skin blistered and ripped and now Auntie G says I have to wait two weeks to do it again. Got to let the skin heal.

> Auntie G: "Jessie, slow and steady wins the race. Think about it and please be careful."

> Me: "My hand hurts."

*
* * Determination *
*

I finally heard back from Bryan Q. Miller! Writer of the best Batgirl ever — Stephanie Brown!

Dear Bryan,

I am so happy that Ricki convinced me to write to you! She's my comic-book source and told me about your work. Like writing for *Batgirl* comics and *Smallville*. I have a school project to investigate super-heroes and we can also include science so I told Mr. Richardson (he's our biology teacher) that I am going to look at really "extreme" human abilities.

I think he imagines the X-Games or something. The truth is that I am looking at the reality of be-coming as slick as Batgirl! I considered all kinds of human superheroes but I think Batgirl is best. Which is where you come in. Or why I am writing to you, I mean.

Because your Stephanie Brown Batgirl was awesome. She's a great character and I love the way you wrote her. I especially like the great talks between Stephanie and Barbara. Or Batgirl and Or-acle. Well both. I think you know what I mean!

Much appreciated—the goal was to make them as close a thing to sisters and friends as possible. They each had something to gain by engaging with the other.

The way you had Steph talk with her mom was also cool. Actually, sounds kind of silly but I just basically liked all the stuff you did in *Batgirl*. So there.

Anyway, sometimes I get off track a bit. Like just now. Yeah. Here are my questions!

Who is your favorite superhero? Is that the same as when you were a teenager like me? (This year I turned 13.)

When I was much younger, it was Spider-Man, hands down. A normal, smart kid with terrible luck who had trouble fitting in, who suddenly found a sort of release and joy in anonymity and superpowers. Now? Superman. Not that I *didn't* love Superman when I was little, but, as an adult, I have a much greater appreciation for everything that he stands for—for the symbol that Superman is. Truth. Justice. Freedom. And (depending on how he's being written) he makes all of that possible with a strong arm, a gentle hand, and a polite smile. He's a symbol for all the greatness humanity can and should achieve . . . and he isn't even one of us. Simply remarkable!

And happy 13!

Do you think Batgirl could ever beat someone as tough as Batman?

I certainly hope she would never be put into that situation. Are we talking physically, mentally, or emotionally? Emotionally, I think Batgirl takes all. Stephanie, for better or worse, faced and accepted her past and self-realized herself into a new stage in life. She knows how important it is to have a community and support system as well and does what she can to maintain it. Batman, not so much. Or, at least, not to where he would admit it. Physically, he's the best of the best and a tank of a man. Hard to beat in a straight fight. Unless someone manages to trap him inside of a giant hourglass or something. ;-)

Did you ever worry about Stephanie's safety when she was out on patrol as Batgirl? She had to fight some pretty bad people.

Yes, which is why it was so important for her to not be afraid to ask for help when she needed it. Like in issue #23, when she knew going in to the prison scenario that she was going to need back-up. And so she set things in motion to get her lady-friends in place ahead of time! Steph is also a very resourceful young woman and doesn't really have any issues with pride. She'll do her best to overcome any obstacle but knows when to fall back and regroup. She's been through too much to ignore the lessons of her past.

Did you always want to be a writer?

I always wanted to be a creator of some sort—whether that be through art, photography, or writing. The bug has always been there to tell stories. Writing is a great way of doing that.

How did you know how to write such a great girl character?

Thanks! The key, really, isn't to write a character as male *or* female—just to write them as a person. "How would a *person* in that character's situation react?" You should never go to a place of "a girl wouldn't say that!" Anyone, of any race, of any sex, can do or say anything. How they behave is based on their past experiences and their current sense of self.

I'm not trying to actually become Batgirl, BTW. But I am trying to get better at stuff in real life. I am doing lots of exercises and taking martial arts lessons from my aunt. Do you have any advice for me?

Though physicality is important for being a hero, never forget that heroes inspire through their actions and deeds, and not just with the throwing of a punch. Heroes are symbols. They inspire. Gandhi was a hero, right? So was Martin Luther King Jr.

Thanks for creating such a great character!

In all fairness, I simply carried the ball downfield—Mr. Chuck Dixon (I believe) gets the Stephanie credit. All the same, thank *you* for going along on the adventure with her!

Oh man! Bryan is so talented. He could do so many different things but chose writing. I think it's so cool the way he talks about writing characters as people — not men or women or girls or boys. And about how heroes and superheroes inspire.

He has inspired me to keep writing, that's for sure!

MONDAY, NOVEMBER 24

* Physical Strength *

OK. Let's get right at it. I've been busy this whole month peppering Mom with questions about the body. Over the years she has done lots of lab tests on all kinds of athletes: ones who row, do judo, or ski. And professional athletes like NHL players from New York, Los Angeles, Edmonton, and Buffalo. She has been busy!

Now I need to get serious about "Building Batgirl's Body." It's basic training for Jessie.

I've been sleuthing out how training will affect my body. Like my muscles, my bones, and even my skin (and maybe how to avoid more blisters in the future!). I don't want my mom directly involved so I've been real sneaky asking her stuff. But I did get her to help me figure out how to do some fitness tests on myself. And Shay helped too. I suspect she thinks it's best to be nice so I give her a decent Christmas present. And so she can get Mom and Dad to think she's been good all year. Not.

The fitness tests will tell me if I'm actually getting stronger and stuff. The Big Bad List of Things Include:

* Number of pushups in a minute
* Number of situps in a minute
* Number of chin-ups I can do (chin-ups are evil, BTW. Pure. Evil.)

* How many seconds I can hold my body up in a chin-up (when the number of chin-ups is less than one, this is, like, microseconds! LOL.)
* How far I can get my fingers past my toes when I'm stretching forward
* How long it takes me to run around the soccer field three times
* How long I can hold a plank position (like from Pilates that we did in gym.)
* How long I can balance on one leg . . . before falling over

I've kept up my rock-climbing class and my karate. Those seem to be pretty good activities for keeping my body in good shape and getting me strong.

Mom says it's good to do many different kinds of activities. She calls it "cross-training"; it can help me (Batgirl) train two (or three or many more) things at once. My mom says that there are lots of different ways to do that. She quite likes "CrossFit." I may give it a try!

I saw this show about the CrossFit Games. They had the women's competition and I just about fell out of my chair. Okay. I was lying on the couch, but still I was startled.

One of the competitors was from Iceland. She won the CrossFit games twice. Which is pretty impressive, but it's not why I fell off the couch. That happened because of her name. But not her first name (Annie), her last name, which is Thorisdottir. That is Icelandic for "Thor's Dottir" = Thor's Daughter! Awesome. Thor!

But anyway, back to me. My muscles do lots of different things. But all of them involve producing force, apparently! But producing large forces — being strong — and producing force while moving quickly — being powerful — are not exactly the same thing, as it turns out.

Batgirl does loads of training. From all the stuff in the comics and my research with Mom, it looks like hours and hours a day would be needed to develop her physique.

And she'd need to keep training all the time to maintain it. She is also a busy high-school student. This means that Batgirl is continually on the go.

No matter what Batgirl does, it involves moving somehow. Fast or slow, lots or little. All of that movement means her muscles are constantly pulling on her bones. So, Batgirl's bones cannot be brittle. Brittle is bad. How do I toughen up my bones?

Question: does Batgirl drink milk? I'm guessing yes.

She'd look funny on one of those ads with the milk mustache on her mask. I prefer chocolate milk, if you're asking. Mom says milk helps strengthen bones as well as muscles.

It seems like Batgirl needs to be really good at all things. Can I be the best at everything, though? Can I be the strongest, fastest, and go the longest? I also need to get more ammo to sling back at Dylan. Maybe Batgirl isn't as strong as Batman, but in some things women can have better stamina than men! That's a tidbit from Mom. I wish I'd known that when Dylan and Audrey were arguing about men and women.

Something my mom said recently really stuck with me: men and women do have different capabilities. But for a long time women weren't even allowed to compete in the same sports as men. So how's it fair to say men were better than women if they didn't even let women train at those sports? Mom says now that women can do all the same sports as men, the difference is getting smaller and smaller.

So there, Dylan.

WEDNESDAY, NOVEMBER 26

My secret Batgirl training is going well. Something I find pretty neat is when I learn how to do some special martial arts move. Like when Auntie G showed me how to escape from a wrist grab. I was, like, yanking and yanking on her hand and arm. And getting NOWHERE. I just could not get free from her grab no matter how hard I tried. Then she showed me how to turn my body and twist my wrist – poof! My hand popped right out of her hand. It was so very cool. Well, it was pulchritudinous.

I keep making lots of mistakes even though I can see I'm getting a bit better! I looked up on the net (brainfacts.org) that the cells in my brain have been changing from all this! Scientists who study the nervous system – who do neuroscience – call this "plasticity" because it gets at the idea of the brain's "changeability." And what is controlling all of that? Turns out different parts of the brain do different things.

A bit way at the back of my head is called·the cerebellum. Kind of looks like cauliflower, but that could just be because I'm hungry! What's weird about the cerebellum is that it's one-tenth of the whole brain but has more than half of the brain cells, a.k.a. neurons!

Since there are like 100 billion neurons in the brain, that means 50 billion are in that little cerebellum. And it turns out that each neuron could have 1,000 or up to 10,000 connections on it! That's 100 trillion connections! Something is definitely going on in there.

I tried to use some of those neurons today in a special test we learned in gym class. We did this reaction time test to see how fast we could respond to something. It was pretty cool – we got to measure time in centimeters!

We got into pairs (I was with Audrey – yay!) and each pair got a ruler. Then we took the ruler and one partner (me) held it hanging down between my thumb and first finger. Then I just let go of the ruler and Audrey was supposed to grab it as quickly as possible between her hands.

Mr. Pratt said that gravity is pulling down on the ruler with a constant force and we could use the distance the ruler traveled as a way to tell how long it took to grab it! Closer to the top means faster!

We each did it three times. The first time Audrey didn't do anything and it dropped right through her hands and hit her foot. We both started laughing. I asked, "How did you manage to even walk to school today?" We were both rolling around laughing for quite a while. Too long, according to Mr. Pratt.

Next time, she got 10 centimeters and then 12 centimeters. This worked out to 0.14 seconds and 0.16 seconds. Which was pretty good. I got 10, 12, and 5. The 5 was actually the best in class and works out to 0.10 seconds.

Mr. Pratt showed us this table:

Excellent	<7.5 cm
Above Average	7.5–15.9 cm
Average	15.9–20.4 cm
Below Average	20.4–28 cm
Poor	>28 cm

I was feeling pretty good about myself after that. Until I got home, that is. I thought I would show little sister Shay how quick on the draw big sister Jessie was. So I did the test with her.

Shay got 6, 7, and 5 for her three tries. She wanted to know if that was any good. I said, yeah it was okay, I guess.

OK. She was looking over my shoulder when I wrote that. She seemed happy enough with "okay" and has moved on to the kitchen to get a snack. Shay is so fast! SHE could actually be Batgirl NOW!

Like Mom is always telling us, we are all naturally more talented at some things than others — so Shay is really fast even though she hasn't been doing any Batgirl training — but others can work hard to be just as good or better.

You can't beat hard work (according to Mom).

I'm still thinking that over . . .

FRIDAY, NOVEMBER 28

* Preparation *

More Batgirl questions: Is it possible to see and hear more than normal? Or smell more? How does Batgirl use her Jedi mind-tricks to fool opponents?

Batgirl's mind — her ability to out-think bad guys — has got to be her best weapon. And her best defense. She needs to train a mind that sees what others overlook, to work all the senses to the maximum, and to unleash her inner superhero-ness.

Training with Auntie G this week I found out a very important thing. Something that a Batgirl-in-training needs to understand. Vision is the queen of our other senses. Like when I'm sitting in our car at a stoplight and another car pulls up beside us. Sometimes when I look over at that other car as it moves forward it feels like our car is moving backward! It's a visual illusion.

Auntie G did this thing where she lined up in front of me in a fighting position. Then she kind of crouched a bit lower. It totally looked like she was shrinking into herself! Anyway, it looked like she was getting further away from me but then — BAM! She jumped right at me and did a kick.

I could not move at all. Her kick came right up and hit me — not too hard, just a tap — right in my tummy. It totally took me by surprise. I had a total reaction fail.

Auntie G said that visual illusions are very powerful. Super-bat-fantastic-powerful. Batgirl knows this and she can use it to her advantage when she is getting herself out of trouble! She knows how to use her movements to delude bad guys (and bad girls). Just like Auntie G showed me.

Next Auntie G says I need to try some exercises that Batgirl would do to help improve her ability to pay attention to the world around her.

I'm tuning up my senses: hearing, seeing, tasting, smelling, and touching.

This sense training stuff is harder than I thought it would be. First up, last Saturday, was smell. To be random, I wrote out all the senses on paper strips and drew them out of a hat. Very high tech. Audrey would have for sure written a whole computer program just to do this!

Anyway, Auntie G said the way to do it is the same with each sense and that I should do one sense per day. As soon as I wake up, I remember which sense I am going to concentrate on that day. And then really focus on it. All day long.

TUESDAY, DECEMBER 9

Today I was supposed to focus on taste, but oops, I forgot all about that when I woke up. I just ate my breakfast without concentrating, which kind of ruined it. I remembered when I was showering but then forgot until after lunch, which was too late to be of any use since I'd already eaten two meals by then. And a snack. And I had some gum too. And mints. Too late, too late, too late. Argh.

So instead of exploring my taste buds — or my "taste bugs" like Shay used to say, so cute! — I explored hearing. I worked really hard to focus on only certain sounds or certain things.

So, when we were in science class, I focused on just trying to hear Mr. Richardson for a change. Ha!

OK. No. Seriously, I usually listen to Mr. Richardson. But today I tried to hear the ticking of the clock. It was pretty cool because it was hard to hear at first but once I heard a bit of a tick, it got easier to hear it more and more. It's like my brain identified it as something important and then I could hear it better.

Unfortunately, while I was busy listening to the clock go tick tock, I really did zone out on Mr. Richardson.

Which made me think of asking Audrey for her notes later.

Which made me think of Audrey.

Which made me look across the class to Audrey.

Which is why I saw Cade leaning forward in his desk whispering something to her.

Which is why I saw her laugh and Cade laugh. But I wasn't part of the "whatever they were laughing about."

Which is why I feel like I'm on the outside looking in.

WEDNESDAY, DECEMBER 10

Argh. Arrgh. Arrrgh. Arrrrrrrrrrrgh! Group assignments!

Normally I'm okay with group assignments. It just depends on the group. Group projects where the teacher assigns the members? Not OK. Argh. I am so glad that the Superhero Slam is solo. Just me and Batgirl.

Because guess who is in my group? Dylan, of course. And, of course, Dylan is driving me to shouting! Group assignments with lazy group members are not my thing! Group assignments where the teacher puts people who don't care with those who do?

Not. Cool.

Yargh. Yargh? What am I, a pirate now? See, diary? That's how frustrated I am. I have to resort to pirate-talk . . . matey.

It's always so brutal when you get randomly assigned to a group. It's me, Jack, and Dylan. Sigh. Jack did okay, but Dylan?!? Whenever we had work time in class for our mini-project on Confucianism — or it felt more like confusionism — all he did was sit there listening to music on his iPod and doodling pictures of, well, I'm not sure what. Some stuff, on his paper, on the desk, basically everywhere. And he isn't particularly skilled at doodling, our Dylan.

I wonder what it's like for Batgirl. A lot of the time she is by herself doing her own thing. But she has to work in groups too. Like with other Bat-Family members Nightwing, Robin, Batman, and others. Or her major Birds of Prey friends like Black Canary, Huntress, and Hawkgirl.

Batgirl couldn't have gotten on great with everybody all the time. But there was always something they had to do, so I guess Batgirl had to figure out a way to do it no matter what. And I guess I do too!

Anyway, we are supposed to finish up our assignment by Monday. So I finally let Dylan have it!

Me: "Hey, Dylan?"

Dylan: "Huh?"

Me: "We have to finish up our assignment. Since you have done, well, basically nothing so far, you are going to finish it up on your own this weekend. Got it?"

Dylan (sighing): "Ya, OK. That seems fair, you guys. I really haven't done much so far."

Jack (looking startled, surprised, and unsure what to say at this shocking turn of events): "?"

Me: "Good."

Pretty good, if I do say so myself. Except I am saying so myself, by myself, to myself because that whole conversation took place in my head. I was so going to tell Dylan off today but I just froze and couldn't do it.

So that means what really happened is it got left for me to pull the assignment together into a fantastic pleasing-to-the-eye poster. Which I — by myself — will work super hard on all weekend. And (of course) it will look great but I am also super frustrated. Why should all that fall to me to do? Uh oh. Here it comes again . . . Yarghhh!

One thing I will say for Dylan, he's at least honest. We have to give ourselves a grade for effort and input, Dylan said he didn't really do anything (true) and just wasn't into it (that is sure how it looked). So he'll get a worse mark than Jack and me. (It's not like I want him to get a worse mark. But I do want to get a mark that I deserve.)

Still, I'd rather get a good mark and not have to work ALL WEEKEND on the assignment. I told Ms. King that too. In fact I told her I'm doing enough work for two assignments.

She just kind of smiled at me and nodded her head. You know, in that way that adults do when they generally agree with what you are saying but aren't going to do anything about it.

At least she kind of grudgingly admitted it and it made me feel a bit better. But I would have felt a lot better if I could've just stood up for myself. When am I going to stand up to Dylan?

OK. Last one: Yarghh!

FRIDAY, DECEMBER 12

Christmas is within touching distance. Only two weeks away. It's almost here! Yay! You know, it really is the most wonderful time of the year! Christmas break is wonderful because everyone's together . . . AND there's no homework. ☺

MONDAY, DECEMBER 15

* Perseverance *
  * & Determination *
        *

Today I got my answer from Jessica Watson! It was so awesome to read her book TRUE SPIRIT: THE TRUE STORY OF A 16-YEAR-OLD AUSTRALIAN WHO SAILED SOLO, NONSTOP, AND UNASSISTED AROUND THE WORLD. And then to write and ask her stuff. And now she has a TRUE SPIRIT movie coming out too!

Dear Jessica,

It is really cool to write to you! I've been doing a lot of research for my project on heroes. My Socials teacher, Ms. King, has been telling us lots about explorers and stuff. It got me looking up women in history and I read about Amelia Earhart and her flying adventures. That's when I came across your story!

It would be great if you could answer some questions.

When you were sailing around the world, did you ever get really lonely? What did you do?
I missed all my family and friends from the moment I sailed out of Sydney and there were times when I was really home sick but I never use the word lonely. Lonely is when all your friends are away and you've got no one to hang out with! It also really helped that there were people from around the world sending me messages of support.

Did you have a favorite song you played?
I didn't really have a favorite song but before I left lots of people gave me CDs of their favorite music, so whenever I would listen to a different CD it would remind me of the person who gave it to me. A song called "Forever Young" got lots of airplay!

Did you ever think about quitting, because it was taking too long or was too difficult? How did you handle that?
It never crossed my mind to stop or give up, there were definitely times when I was asking myself why on earth I was

doing it, but I could always answer my own question. Always staying positive was so important!

What was the scariest thing that happened to you? What about the most surprising?

The scariest thing that happened on the voyage was when *Pink Lady* was rolled upside down four times in one night by huge waves in the Atlantic Ocean.

One of the most surprising things that happened was having a dolphin swim along next to *Pink Lady* for six hours during a storm; it was just like the dolphin was looking after us!

What was the hardest thing that happened?

There were some really hard times sailing, but the hardest thing of all was actually all the hard work and preparation I had to do before I left.

What does it feel like to know you accomplished something as epic as sailing around the world by yourself?

It's an amazing feeling to achieve your dream! I taught myself that if I work hard and really set my mind to something, I can achieve anything I want to!

Do you have a favorite superhero?

I'm not sure I really have a favorite superhero? I don't think you have to have superpowers to achieve amazing things; we can all do amazing things if we believe in ourselves!

The way Jessica describes her journey almost makes it seem like no big deal! But I looked up the distances again, and I can't get over what an amazing journey it was — 23,000 nautical miles over seven months. That's so awesome! That's like if I went back and forth between New York and Los Angeles six times! By myself!

And Jessica is so positive and sure of herself. One of the things I've figured out so far is that if you really want to achieve something, you need to be pretty determined.

And never ever give up.

Yay! Great Christmas! After dinner, I asked Auntie G my question about bones. She had an answer I wasn't expecting. She said that a long time ago martial artists wanted to toughen up their bones.

The old martial arts masters knew even way back then that bones in the legs seemed stronger than those in the arms. Auntie G (and Mom chimed in too) said that this was because we bang our legs into the ground all the time. It's called walking and running! And all that banging makes our bones get strong. Since we don't bang our hands and arms into the ground all the time, those bones aren't as strong.

But training in judo, which has loads of grabbing, grappling, and throwing, and in karate, which involves a lot of punching, kicking, and striking, makes for stronger bones throughout the body.

That all fits with the picture of my body adjusting to what I do, which Mom and Auntie G have been talking about. But I want to make my bones stronger on purpose. Like for my arms, would I need to be a street performer or work in the circus doing a show where I walk on my hands?

Nope. Auntie G said they used to do a thing called body hardening back in China at the Shaolin Temple and in Okinawa. And some other places. And when she explained it to me, I really see why it's called body hardening, all right.

Basically you bash your body into hard stuff! Yikes. Seriously, punching hard objects like trees and stuff will make your bones stronger. And your skin thicker apparently. And it would make you generally pretty tough, I think!

To see this taken pretty far, Auntie G told me about this guy named — and I'm really not making this up — Iron Fist. It's his actual nickname. Marvel Comics even has a martial arts superhero named Iron Fist too.

The real-life Iron Fist is a Chinese martial arts master who trains his hands every day. He's got, like, this huge set of gross calluses all over his one fist! Yikes.

I looked him up online. His hand is MASSIVE. But just the ONE hand. The other looks pretty normal.

Random hero factoid: In an AVENGERS story called "Superguardian," this grandpa guy tells his granddaughter, "Heroes make others believe they can do great things. Heroes make heroes." It's amazing to think you could do something in your life that would inspire others. It's like what Bryan Q. Miller said about superheroes as symbols. Like Gandhi inspiring social change in India and Martin Luther King Jr. in the American Civil Rights movement.

Inspiration is contagious. Batgirl didn't start out as a superhero. She was inspired and trained by Batman. Superheroes make superheroes. Basically, Batman helped make Batgirl.

SATURDAY, JANUARY 10

*
* Physical Strength *
*   & Agility *

Mom says I've been turning into a bit of an athlete now that I've upped my martial arts practice to three days per week. I go to Auntie G's class on Mondays and Wednesdays and then she does some special one-on-one with me on Saturday mornings.

I am pretty lucky, actually. My teacher comes right to me! (Pretty sure Batgirl didn't have Batman swing by her apartment for training!) On weekends, we train in my backyard. Usually she likes to work on fighting drills and footwork with me. Then she goes for a run with my mom after. I guess it is pretty much family bonding day, now that I think of it.

Auntie G is so into training me! I think she's been secretly waiting for me to get interested in martial arts. Plus I must be pretty cool to work with. If the definition of cool includes not being that good at something and having to be taught the same thing over and over again.

Today's big focus was on getting out of the way. Like when somebody (a bad guy) is trying to attack me. I did okay but I had a bit of a fail at first.

> Auntie G: "Great, Jess, that was good. Now what do you do when somebody bad comes at you and tries to hit you or grab you or whatever?"
>
> Me: "Um . . . get away?" (I said it kind of weakly, I have to be honest about that.)

113

Auntie G: "O-kay, but where are you going to go that's 'away'?"

Me: "I think . . . backward? Yeah. Backing up is away, right?"

Auntie G: "Yes, it is away, sort of. But you are still right in front of me. Here, let's try it."

And then Auntie G started chasing me all over the place with kicks and punches and strikes and lunges and I just kept trying to back up – fast – and get away. Except my plan only got me stuck against a tree.

Auntie G: "OK. Now what? What have you learned?"

Me: "Well." (I was huffing and puffing pretty good at this point.) "I guess I give up and I've learned that you are scary-faster than me."

Auntie G: "Of course I'm faster than you; I've been doing this for a long time. You will get faster too! But I want to talk about this 'give up' stuff. There is no give up when somebody wants to hurt you. There is no stop or 'I quit.' OK?"

Me: "OK. But how do I not get in this situation in the first place? I was trying my hardest to get away."

Auntie G: "Let's change it from getting away to getting OUT OF the way, all right? When you think of it like that, hopefully you see that backing up doesn't get out of the way, even if you're putting some distance between us. Let's try again with you hook stepping your legs and rotating out of the way and slide stepping out of the way like we've practiced. If you are doing it right, I won't be able to just attack you again, because you won't still be standing right in front of me. I'll have to move."

So we practiced it again. And again, and again, and again. Let's just say, we did it many, many times! She was very patient with me. Once I was doing a bit better, Auntie G went on to explain to "always try to escape. But you have to plan it and get out of the way, be in a good position to do something like hit your attacker, and then get away."

"Safety first makes you last!" was the final bit of advice for the day. Auntie G thought she was being super hilarious. It was funny. Sort of.

I can't believe how good it felt to be able to do that. It's hard to believe I'm able to do this kind of thing, because I'm always having difficulty getting my body to do what I want!

But by the end of practice today, if I'd had a mask and cape on, I might've easily been mistaken for Batgirl! ☺

MONDAY, JANUARY 12

I'm Batgirl! I mean in the Slam! Today was the day we had to declare which superhero we are going to be in

the Superhero Slam. There were a couple of surprises when Ms. King had everyone announce their superheroes.

Mine was Batgirl, of course. Audrey said Iron Man (no big surprise either) and Cade went with Aquaman. What a shocker. Mr. Swimmer goes with the ultimate swimming superhero! Does Cade think he can just swim to a win? ☺

The biggest surprise came from the usual corner – Dylan. And should I have expected anything different from him, really? Dylan, my nemesis, my nightmare. Who did he choose? He chose Batman! Batman, can you believe it?

I just sat in class stunned by Dylan's choice. Does he realize Batman's a HERO, not a VILLAIN? Did he actually mean to choose the Joker or Two-Face or Penguin or something but forgot what he was doing and made a mistake? Ugh.

I can't believe his superhero is Batman. Batman is all about hard work, training, and helping others. Just like Batgirl.

Hard work and helping is so not Dylan. He's all about coasting, being lazy, and doing as little as possible.

He CANNOT win the Superhero Slam!

He MUST not win!

It would be morally wrong! Yargh!

TUESDAY, JANUARY 13

* Preparation *

I am going nuts about nutrition. Apparently nuts are good things to eat, so it's kind of funny what I wrote just now. Or maybe it's not. Whatever. This is my diary.

Or journal.

Or non-blog log.

So I can

    pretty

        much

            do

            whatever

            I

        want

    here.

And what I want to do is get a little more serious about what I eat.

Since I'm doing so much physical activity, I am a lot hungrier a lot more of the time. I also noticed there's less food around the house for me to snack on . . . because I snacked on it already!

So I asked Mom about what real athletes eat. She told me if I wanted an extreme example, to go check out what Michael Phelps used to eat when he was swimming up a storm.

So I did.

Incredible! He said he ate like 12,000 calories a day while training for the 2008 Summer Olympics. An average guy his age might eat about 2,000 calories. Yikes. But he was swimming and training hours every day so he was using up lots of energy.

Gets me wondering how much food it takes to be an active teen like Batgirl and how many calories she would use up. You know, if she were a real person.

Mom showed me a website that would give me an idea of how much energy I use every day. She said that to really do this properly I'd need to come into her lab. But this website was a good estimate.

I'm not sure I would've found that site on my own. Mom had to tell me to search for "basal metabolic rate." Anyway, there's also all kinds of other calculators out there!

I put in my height (5-foot-5), my weight (130 lbs), and my age (13) and then presto the calculator said . . . drumroll please . . . 1464.9 calories. Sweet. Mom said that's the amount of calories I need to eat every day just so my body stays as it is. Without any activity. Like, no gym, no karate, no climbing, no nothing extra. To just stay alive, basically.

Mom said my calories every day would go up (or down)

based on how active (or not) I am. She told me to times my number by 1.7, since I am so active every day. That means about 2,500 calories a day. Cool. Exactly how much energy Batgirl uses depends on what she is up to that day (or night!).

She's drawn a bit bigger than me in lots of the comics and for sure she's more active. She could easily use up to 3,000 calories each day. To stay in balance, Batgirl needs to consume the right amount of food on those days.

Here are three ridiculous things Batgirl could eat to get those 3,000 calories:

> 6 burgers (6 x 500 calories)
> 30 small apples (30 x 100 calories)
> 15 small chocolate bars (15 x 200 calories)

Anyway, just like there have been many different Batgirls, there really are many healthy body types and sizes. But Mom showed me one thing for sure – for the best athletic performance, thin is weak!

And models' and movie stars' bodies aren't often so healthy. Like any teen (and actually people of any age), sometimes Batgirl (and me too!) might be tempted to slip into impulse eating when things aren't going well.

But Batgirl knows that ice cream won't freeze her problems. But Mr. Freeze? That is a different problem entirely.

THURSDAY, JANUARY 22

* * * Preparation * *

I totally love junk food — huge weakness for cotton candy and caramel corn over here. But not together at the same time! Although, now that I think about it that COULD work . . .

But I've seen enough shows to know that a true athlete like Batgirl would need to eat right. Or eat healthy, I guess. My parents have always been on about "healthy eating" and healthy food choices. We get to eat lots of good stuff too, but we're supposed to think about the choices we make.

My parents are totally against soft drinks though. Just "sugar bombs in water," they are always saying. (Sugar bomb doesn't sound that bad to me, actually, but I understand what they mean. Mostly.)

But I never did understand why it was such a big deal. Until Mr. Pratt talked about it in gym today. He was all like "everybody likes sugar," even rats and monkeys.

He showed this video of an experiment somebody did with some rats. He said we were talking about A SERIOUS HEALTH ISSUE.

These rats were just normal happy rats that ate their normal "tasty" rat food. Of course, the rat food was pellets of stuff that, honestly, didn't look so yummy to me but they seemed to just totally love it. Which is the important thing. But when the scientists gave the rats a sugar snack, they just went completely berserk. And wanted to eat sugar all the time.

Mr. Pratt said that when food gets digested and broken down, a lot of it gets burned up or metabolized as a sugar. But it's how that is packaged up that's very important. I don't know if it's because it's so soon after Christmas or what, but Mr. Pratt was all about gift-wrapping and sweets today!

In Mr. Pratt's story, the packaging controls how sugar gets used up in the body. It's all about how it's wrapped up. If the sugar is packaged real flimsy and easy to open, like some thin wrapping paper over a present, you kind of rip it open quickly and get the sugar fix. That's like sugar in soft drinks. Fast acting and super big response.

Instead, if the sugar is packaged up really tightly, it takes way longer to get into the body. If sugar gets into our bodies too fast, the hormones that take care of sugar overreact. Mr. Pratt talked about the two hormones we heard about from Mr. Richardson when he explained diabetes – insulin and glucagon. Insulin helps get sugar into cells and glucagon helps unpack that sugar and send it moving around the body and into other cells.

He said that big sugary drinks make insulin levels go bonkers. And that if you have too much bonkers activity like that, your cells can stop responding to your normal insulin levels and you can wind up with what happens in diabetes! Yikes. The kind of confusing part is that it isn't just the amount of sugar — like the number of calories — it's the way it's packaged up. So a 200-calorie soft drink and a 200-calorie snack of apple and banana doesn't do the same thing to insulin levels. The sugar in the fruit is wrapped in a tighter package.

Mr. Pratt said it's kind of like when your younger sister or brother keeps bugging you all the time. Eventually you just start to ignore them. My inside voice wanted to suggest that sometimes, instead of ignoring them you just slug them. But of course I didn't say that out loud because I try never to talk in class, and anyway, by the way Mr. Pratt was acting about our SERIOUS HEALTH ISSUE, I didn't think he'd appreciate my sense of humor. When Mr. Pratt is talking about A SERIOUS HEALTH ISSUE, it is best to pay attention and be quiet. Unless, that is, you want to seriously improve your health by TAKING A REALLY LONG RUN.

Which brings me to Auntie G. She'll be here in a few minutes for my one-on-one martial arts lesson. We're doing it today because she's away this weekend. She warned me that I'll be tired after tonight because we're doing a bunch of kicking and punching for cardio. Still have time for a snack, but after writing this entry I guess I'll pass on the leftover piece of chocolate cake (sigh) and go for the banana instead.

That way I won't let down Mr. Pratt or Batgirl. ☺

FRIDAY, JANUARY 23

I caught up with Cade and Audrey today at the end of school. Sort of. They've both been away at a school swim meet for the past two days and got back just before the final bell.

Cade won two medals! A gold in the 100 meters and a bronze in the 400-meter freestyle. Awesome! He's such a great athlete. I wish he'd have chosen Batman, instead of Dylan getting him for the Slam.

Audrey didn't win any medals, but she came fourth in her two swim events. Since it's her first year of competitive swimming, that's impressive!

Cade said he was really zoning in on his Aquaman mystique and Audrey's done some more research into building real exoskeletons. Her drawings are amazing. She is going to change the world one day.

I caught them both up on what they missed in P.E. yesterday. I made sure to emphasize the SERIOUS HEALTH ISSUE. I also told them about how much Olympic swimmers in training actually eat.

Cade (blushing?): "Hey, that's not that much! I usually bring three sandwiches for lunch at swim meets!" And then out of nowhere Audrey punched him on the arm.

Audrey: "I thought you said it was an extra one for me and I could eat it? You must be starving; you only got two sandwiches for lunch today."

Cade (rubbing his arm a little but mostly looking at Audrey): "Um. No, it's fine. The muffin you gave me helped out!"

Me: "Anyway, I've found out some pretty cool stuff for my Batgirl reality training. Auntie G was showing me some cool karate moves for getting away by being out of the way!"

I was pretty excited to share with my pals but they were kind of distracted.

> Audrey (not responding to me but instead talking to Cade): "That was awesome when you pulled away from the second-place swimmer in the front crawl! He was really strong!"

> Cade (also not responding to me and instead responding to Audrey): "Yeah, it was pretty hard. He used to always beat me last year. I thought for sure you were going to get bronze in your last race. You almost caught up to the girl in third! Next meet I bet you will take her."

> Me: "Um. OK. See you guys? I guess?"

Seriously friends, obsess much? There's more to life than swimming, you know!

Well, we'll see what everyone says in June when I've won the Superhero Slam AND got some super Batgirl skills under my belt!

MONDAY, FEBRUARY 9

* Determination *   All my research into Batgirl, girl superheroes, and men versus women got me really wondering about women in different sports. Billie Jean King was quite the pioneer in tennis but women have played tennis for a while. What ladies haven't done as much is play ice hockey! So I guess this is my "wick"-ed interview, because I got a letter back from Hayley Wickenheiser!

Dear Hayley,

My aunt and my parents all think you are an awesome athlete. They are really into athletes, especially those – like you – who are super at more than one activity. I know you are an amazing hockey player, because I've watched some Olympic and World Championship games with you starring in them!

But when my Auntie G told me you were also a member of Canada's national softball team at the 2000 Summer Olympics in Sydney, Australia, that was news to me! So I did some research and found out you were the second woman to be in both the Winter and Summer Olympics! And the first ever to play two team sports. And then in 2003, you were the first woman to score a goal in the Finnish men's professional hockey league! And you have multiple Olympic and World Championship gold medals in hockey! Wow.

I am doing a big school project about super-heroes, training, and human ability – especially about girls' ability. I've been looking into whether you could actually train to become Batgirl. Some of my classmates think that boys are better at sports than girls are. I don't agree, but I have learned that it is often a lot harder for girls to do some things. Or get the chance to do some things.

Since you seem to have gone after your dreams, I was hoping you could answer some questions about your life in sports.

Hi, Jessie. Thanks so much for your letter. That sounds like an awesome school project, and I totally think you could train to become Batgirl (although I'm not sure about the costume, I'd change that). I believe that you should always go after your dreams, no matter how high or how hard they seem—that just makes you try harder! I'll do my best at answering your questions.

I read that you started playing hockey at age five. How did you get interested in hockey in the first place? Did you get into softball at the same time?
I grew up in a family of hockey enthusiasts in a small town filled with even more hockey enthusiasts! Everyone in my family played hockey, and I grew up on the backyard rink pretending to be playing with Gretzky and Messier! My brother, sister, and I would each take turns being different players. I started softball about the same time because my parents believed that it was important to take a break from hockey. So in the summers, we'd play softball. The soul of our community was rooted in the two sports and it just made sense to be a part of that.

What was it like to play on boys' teams when you were a kid? And what was it like to play hockey on the men's team in Finland? Did the boys get any smarter or nicer?
Growing up playing on boys' teams and playing against other boys' teams wasn't easy. I was so happy I got the chance to play hockey and, for the most part, the boys on my team were pretty good, but the parents seemed to have a harder time with it. I changed in the bathrooms instead of the locker rooms so at times I didn't feel as

tight as the rest of the team. I did seem to have a target on my back—but I've been told that it wasn't just because I was a *girl*, it was also because I was good. I had more to prove, and there were tears of frustration and hurt feelings along the way, but it just made me push even harder!

The older "boys" in Finland were great, though there is always a sense that I have more to prove. The biggest difference there was the power and muscle capacity of the men—there are some differences in physiology between men and women. But all my life those differences in physiology has made me push harder to grow stronger and stay in top form, so I can compete.

So far, what has been the biggest challenge in your life? How did you deal with it?

I think the biggest challenge for me (and you may be surprised to hear this!) is overcoming bad losses, like when Canada won silver at the 1998 Olympics in Japan. When I go out to play, and especially when I'm representing my home country, I play to win. And when that doesn't happen, it is really hard for me.

At the 2013 World Championship in Ottawa, we lost in the gold medal round to the U.S.A. I had hurt my back in this tournament, which was related to a knee injury that I thought had healed enough, so this loss seemed personal. I felt, to some degree, responsible. It isn't because I think I carry the team—not by a long shot. Our team is amazing, but in that game the pieces just did not fit together. It's easier to take the loss when you know you played your best and gave it your all.

Another challenge in my life is time management.

Outside of being a full-time athlete, I'm also going to school to become a doctor and I'm also a mom to my amazing son, Noah. Juggling the time to study (and I have to study hard!), making dinner, training, driving Noah to swim practice, and so on is a daily struggle. I overcome this challenge by learning how to manage my time: making lists, keeping accountable to others, and having support through family, friends, and professionals.

Have you had any big injuries and how did you work through them?

My most recent injury, as I mentioned above, was my back spasms during the 2013 World Championship in Ottawa. At the 2006 Olympics in Turin, I played the gold medal game with a broken hand! I have to honestly admit that I don't deal well with injury. When you are a professional athlete and something stops you from doing what you love, it is very frustrating.

I am so fortunate to have an amazing team of trainers and therapists from Hockey Canada and my own personal trainers who are excellent with treatment and rehabilitation. They help to guide me through the rest and heal stage, because that is the hardest! You have to be certain that your body is able to handle getting back on the ice without injuring yourself more.

If you go out too early, your body will tell you loud and clear!

When I told my Socials teacher that I was going to write to you, she got super excited. She said you "really support the community" and then she told me about your work with KidSport, Right to Play, and

Plan Canada's Because I Am a Girl. How did you get involved with those organizations?

I have always believed in the power and responsibility of giving back to the community and want to support organizations that align with my beliefs. I also know how hard it was growing up as a girl in a male-dominated sport, so I want to be able to help girls today overcome some of those barriers.

That passion for youth in sport naturally led me to these great organizations. My career naturally allows me to connect with girls and women not only across Canada but also around the world.

I truly believe that self-confidence and inner strength find outer expression when girls are empowered through sport.

You have an awesomely ridiculous number of gold and silver medals! (Great work, by the way!) What do you do with all of those medals?

I bring my medals with me when I speak at or visit schools. I believe I share the medals with all Canadians, so I want everyone to be able to see, touch, and experience them. I know athletes who keep their medals locked up, but I'd rather let people see them and be inspired by the story of how I got them—the journey is so much more important than the hardware.

Do you have a favorite superhero?

I'd have to say Superman. Possibly because of his superhuman strength and speed, and that X-ray vision is pretty cool. I wish I had that!

Awesome! I will totally show this letter to Cade and Audrey! (If I can track them down, that is.) They will be totally jazzed. I'd like to show it to Dylan to see the jealous look on his face, but I won't bother. I'm going to show him something else, instead: defeat at the Superhero Slam!

Yep. I am very brave writing in this journal. But will I have the courage of Hayley Wickenheiser in real life?

WEDNESDAY, FEBRUARY 11

*
* Critical Thinking *
        *

Today Ms. King told us about a few really special women in history. One was Joan of Arc, who I have to say I had never heard of before. I didn't feel too bad though, because nobody else had ever heard of her either.

OK. Not totally true. Dylan said he had read about Joan of Arc before. And he looked serious. Just when I think I have him all figured out, he completely surprises me.

Here's my summary of the life and times of Joan of Arc!

Joan was born over 600 years ago in the town of Domrémy in France. When she was a young girl, she started hearing voices in her head telling her she could be the warrior to save France in the 100 Years War with England. When Joan was 15 years old, she ran away from home and, after working really hard to prove herself, got to be captain of the French army and led the forces into battle!

Apparently she was a huge hit, an inspirational leader, and she won a bunch of battles. Unfortunately, she eventually lost a battle and got captured by the English as a prisoner of war. She got charged with all kinds of things and went through a trial that lasted more than a year. She was killed in 1431 at the age of 19. It really was a tragic and bleak finish for Joan of Arc, actually.

Pretty powerful stuff. When my inner voice tells me to do something, it's usually about sneaking another cookie as a snack! Or perhaps reaching out and flicking Shay on the ear and pretending I didn't do anything while we are sitting watching TV. And then rolling on the floor in mock pain when she hits me back followed by protesting my innocence to Mom and Dad. Not that I EVER have done that.

Well, today I didn't. At least not YET.

Seriously, that must have been so tough for Joan to try and get people to listen to her but have them ignore her (mostly) just because she was a girl. But she kept pushing and pushing and trying and doing until they had no choice but to listen to her. Maybe that's how I can get my voice heard. Just keep pushing!

Ms. King ended our class today by saying, "Joan of Arc was inspired to try and change the world. Think about

that and then ask yourself: what have I done lately?"
What would we do to help the world if we had our
superpowers, like, for real?

> What I would do if I really was Batgirl
> * Save people from danger.
> * Train other girls to help me.
> * Scare Dylan into being a nicer person.
> * Hang out with Wonder Woman (I might not
>   want to BE her, but she's still pretty cool).
> * Ask Superman to take me for a flight over my
>   city.
> * Other stuff that I will think of later . . . probably.

Hmm. I don't know how I'd ever figure out the first item
— save people from danger.

Like, what is dangerous enough to be "danger"? People
getting robbed? People almost walking into traffic?
People just about to get into a fight? People in a fight?
And which people? Kids? Adults? Old ladies?

How do I decide what to do? It would be hard to
actually decide who gets help and who doesn't. No
wonder Spider-Man is always so torn. He struggles
all the time with that "with great power comes great
responsibility" line.

I always thought that the responsibility part meant
actually saving people who were obviously in danger. I
didn't really think at all about having to decide who to
save, when to save them, where is the greatest need
for saving, and how to decide.

I asked Mom what she thought. Not about Spider-Man,

but about priorities in saving people.

> Me: "So, I've been thinking about superheroes and heroes. And how a hero could actually decide who to save and when to save them . . ."

> Mom: "And?"

> Me: "And I am kind of stuck and right now if I were an actual superhero, I would be standing here trying to figure out what to do and when to do it and I would wind up saving nobody. Which wouldn't be ideal. I wonder if you have any ideas?"

> Mom: "Well, there's those lines you hear in movies all the time, or the older movies anyway. There's a really famous saying, 'Women and children first,' which was supposed to have been used during the sinking of the TITANIC back in 1912. The idea was to make sure that women and children got off the ship and into lifeboats before the men did."

> Me: "Huh. I get the children part, but it seems kind of weird to include women first, doesn't it?"

> Mom: "Yes, it does. I think the real point is to try and first help out those who need help the most. Like someone who is injured, or really old and having trouble getting around, or young children who can't do much for themselves."

After that, Mom went back to the stuff she was working on and I wandered off to my room.

To think.

And I think the answer is saving the people who are in the most danger and can't do anything to save themselves.

Spider-Man's gig is a lot tougher than he gets credit for.

THURSDAY, FEBRUARY 12

* * Determination * *

I sure am getting tired of all this work! How do athletes keep pushing themselves? They must have some serious inspiration for all the perspiration. How does Batgirl force herself forward when fatigue sets in?

It seems that achieving membership in the extended Bat-Family is all about effort and training. About digging deep inside and striving to be successful despite the odds.

Like Gramma used to say, "Kiddo, if life hands you lemons, make lemonade." I used to say, "I don't like lemonade. Can I make iced tea instead?" and it always made her laugh. But now I get it. And Batgirl must understand as well. She can rip lemons in two with her bare hands.

Project Superhero is a long-term project that should go way beyond grade 8! My idea to actually try out a bunch of the training and experiences Batgirl would need has really changed me already.

Once Superhero Slam is over at the end of the school year, I can't see myself going straight back to Little Miss Sits There and Only Reads Comics. I'm proud of being a girl and getting active and with what I've been able to do. I like asking questions and getting answers — even if it's hard work sometimes.

Probably the neatest thing (and I just looked over my shoulder to make sure Mom or Dad aren't here to read this) is that I like doing things. Even if they are hard. That's part of what makes it great.

But I'm not ready for Mom or Dad to know that. Their idea of being active or doing chores or challenging yourself gets all jumbled up in some weird way. And when it comes to housework and chores, when those are hard, I still don't like doing them.

When I'm working hard on the Superhero Slam or my own project, the learning and training feel great! It's different from working hard on chores or homework because it's my choice.

The funny thing is that when I choose to work hard at something, it's actually easier to do!

MONDAY, FEBRUARY 16

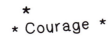 It's all about respect. In karate class, Auntie G said we need to be respectful of others. But to do that we need to have respect for ourselves first. Which is harder to do than it might sound.

But I liked the way she talked about it and how she explained things. She used the "W.I.T.S." thing I learned way back in grade 2!

The old acronym of "walk away," "ignore," "talk about it," "seek help" jazz. Auntie G said we need to always remember the idea of W.I.T.S. But then she did something new with "seek help."

Auntie G said that we don't just seek help from other people, like a parent or teacher or whoever. We have to be able to seek help from ourselves. If nobody else is around, I'm all I've got. And that means being aware of what I can do.

Auntie G also talked about "fear biters." Which made all of us in her class laugh a bit, because it brought up images of little dogs. And that was kind of her point. Any animal will bite if it gets scared. Even the nicest pet can bite its owners if it gets cornered and frightened. I remember that Coco nipped Shay pretty good once. Shay was running around chasing Coco, but she got her backed into a corner in the basement. Coco had nowhere to go and got scared and then bit her.

Coco didn't mean it though and licked Shay and me afterwards. But she was obviously scared in the moment. Well, Auntie G said an animal gets scared because it doesn't have any other choices or options if it gets cornered. So it bites in order to get away.

It's the same with people, said Auntie G. If we think we don't have any options, we are more likely to lash out in fear and anger. Training in martial arts can help give us confidence to know we have other options. And the confidence to make choices that allow us to make use of those other options.

That way we can make sure we AREN'T fear biters and keep a look out for bullies and bad people. But we can learn how to handle them if some find us.

Speaking of fear (but not so much speaking about biting), I just finished reading a chapter in THE DARING BOOK FOR GIRLS called "The Daring Girls Guide to Danger." I think there should be a "!" after Danger or maybe two or three: DANGER!!! BEWARE! DOOM!

Anyway, the authors talk about how facing down some of your fears can be a great thing to try out. They list eight things to do. Some I have already done, and a couple I am keen to try!

* Have a scary movie fest at home.

This one sounds cool and I am working on plans as we speak. So far the top three (three movies in one night is really probably enough) are: THE EXORCIST, THE RING, and JAWS. Dad loves scary movies (he suggested THE RING or THE SHINING), but I don't think Shay will be joining us. Or invited either, if you want to get right down to it.

* Stand up for somebody.

This is a great one. It is pretty nerve wracking when you oppose somebody else. Because you stand out, right? But what's the good of having courage if you don't use it to help out somebody, including yourself!

That's going to be one of my challenges — draw on my courage and do something I never thought I could. Probably that's what being a hero is all about. Doing something even when you are scared. Included on that list is debating in front of the whole class for the Superhero Slam!

SATURDAY, FEBRUARY 21

I thought watching scary movies would be a cool idea.
So I invited Audrey over for a Friday night sleepover.
Mom thought three movies was a bit much for one
night, so we put the names of my top three into a hat
and then picked two: JAWS and THE RING.

And then we got sleeping bags out in the downstairs TV
room, made some popcorn, and settled in for the Scare
Fest. Or we almost settled in. Audrey did a bunch of
texting before we got started. So I was kind of bored
and texted Cade. But he was super slow in answering
some of my brilliant text messages, so I gave up after
a while.

Finally we started watching JAWS. Audrey chose it to
start our Scare Fest because "it would have swimming
scenes." I swear, she and Cade are OBSESSED with

swimming! It had some creepy bits — that music really gets to you. But the shark looked pretty fake, so Audrey and I were able to cover our little bits of fear with lots of laughter.

Which turned out to be kind of a problem because when we went to watch THE RING we were pretty arrogant. We thought it would be silly-scary like JAWS.

We were wrong. Really, really wrong.

THE RING is veryveryveryveryvery scary. The weird way things move around on the screen creeped me right out. And creeped out Audrey too. But we made a pact to finish the movie anyway, and we got all the way through to the end.

When I say "finish the movie," I mean that Audrey and I were in the same room as the TV. But we were buried underneath as many pillows and blankets as we could find and only kind of watching with one eye.

But we did it. Sort of. That took courage, right?

Random factoid: The word "hero" comes from the Greek language. In Greek "heros" means doing something selfless. A real hero could be someone who does something without thinking of themselves or any benefit or reward for doing it. Taking action puts them at risk and may only benefit someone else.

SUNDAY, FEBRUARY 22

Holy Science Action, Batman! Audrey has gone berserk working so hard on her Iron Man project. And reading everything she can get her hands or eyes on about prosthetics. Things you can use to help you if you are injured. Like if you lose a leg in an accident and get an artificial or prosthetic leg to use.

What she's been most fascinated with are "neuroprosthetics." These are connected to your brain or spinal cord or muscles to control devices. Anyway, I guess there was a big show on TV tonight about it. I missed it, but Audrey saw it.

Anyway, she phoned me right after and was, like, talking so fast and was so crazy excited. The show reported on people learning how to control robot arms. Which sounded cool, but not anything that should have gotten Audrey as excited as she was. What's so different about that than just playing a video game and controlling something?

When I said that to Audrey, you could tell by her voice she was having a hard time answering me. Was I from another planet or something? Then she added a point

I didn't get at first. But it is pretty important. People were learning to use their brains to control the robot arms. Say what, say what?

Audrey explained that some professor guys in Pittsburgh took ideas that they had been working on for years on monkeys and got them to work in people. Audrey said one of the scientists named Andy Schwartz did a bunch of research where they connected robot arms to computers and then the computers to the brains of monkeys.

They used wires to grab activity in the monkey brain when the monkeys tried to move their arms. But they used that activity from the brain to control a computer robot arm. I looked it up online and found some incredible videos. One monkey could even feed itself an orange with a robot hand.

Now the scientists are doing this stuff in people with the help of a neurologist named Geoffrey Ling. He did surgery on people with problems in their brains where they couldn't move their arms anymore. So the scientists hooked the computer connection into the brain and then the patients could use a robot hand as if it was their own hand!

Which is cool but also kind of freaky. Because of what they learned from those monkey experiments they could also help people! Like Mom always says, "People are animals too."

A woman on the show who had the implant was named Jan. She actually shook the reporter's hand with her robot thoughts! Or, I mean, her robot hand controlled by her human thoughts shook the reporter's hand.

And of course, Audrey and I realized right away that this was just like what Doctor Octopus was doing in the Spider-Man comics. He has those crazy tentacle arms coming off his back. Doc Ock has wires put into his brain to control his arms. I never knew that some of that was actually possible!

Audrey would so love to do that kind of stuff! (I mean the robot arms to help people, not to become a supervillain.)

Audrey is on track to be an inventor, for sure. But the most important thing is that Audrey is uber-excited about robotics and strong women scientists and inventors! It's SO GOOD to have my pal back to her old self! She is also coming up with lots of great stuff for the Superhero Slam about how Iron Man helps society.

My DARING BOOK FOR GIRLS has a whole list of inventors. One that is super relevant to Batgirl and the extended Bat-Family is Stephanie Louise Kwolek, a chemist. In 1964 she invented Kevlar. It's used everywhere nowadays, in police and military vests, helmets, rackets, and all kinds of stuff. Including the Batsuit, where a polymer fiber five times stronger than steel is a great thing to sew with!

Mary Phelps Jacob invented the modern bra in 1913 while she was still a teenager! She got sick and tired of WEARING A CORSET! Thankfully.

I know I'm not going to be an inventor. Or at least not an inventor of a real product that people can use and which changes the world. But if I do become a journalist, maybe I can help share ideas with people that will change how they think. That can help change the world too!

Yeah, maybe that's how I'll help change the world. With my words.

FRIDAY, MARCH 6

*
* Superhero Slam *
    *   Match-Ups! *

Superhero. Slam.

Today we set up the knockout bracket for the Superhero Slam. Ms. King had us each write our superhero on a recipe card and we then put them into a hat. She then had Mr. Richardson come in to draw names out to pair up all 16 teams. The winner of each debate will be determined by class vote and Ms. King's vote. The only limitation is you can't vote on your own match.

Based on the cards pulled out of the hat, Ms. King wrote out the tournament bracket.

Here's the lineup!

On the one side of the bracket we have:

> Batgirl vs. Green Lantern;
> Captain America vs. Wonder Woman;
> Black Canary vs. Aquaman;
> and Thor vs. Superman.

On the other side:

> Iron Man vs. Storm;
> Invisible Girl vs. Daredevil;
> The Flash vs. Spider-Woman;
> and Elektra vs. Batman.

This is a pretty interesting set up! Audrey and I are on separate sides of the bracket. So if we keep winning, we have a chance at a straight-up duel on whether Batgirl could beat Iron Man! But Cade's on the same side as me, so we could wind up against each other too.

Dylan is lined up on Audrey's side. She has to beat him to get through to the final. Ordinarily I'd say no problem, but Dylan has me worried. I cannot figure him out — can anyone?

Still don't know what he is up to by choosing Batman. But I'll have to just put that out of my mind. I need to make sure my brain is fully focused on making a plan for why and how Batgirl could and should beat Green Lantern!

SUPERHERO SLAM BRACKET

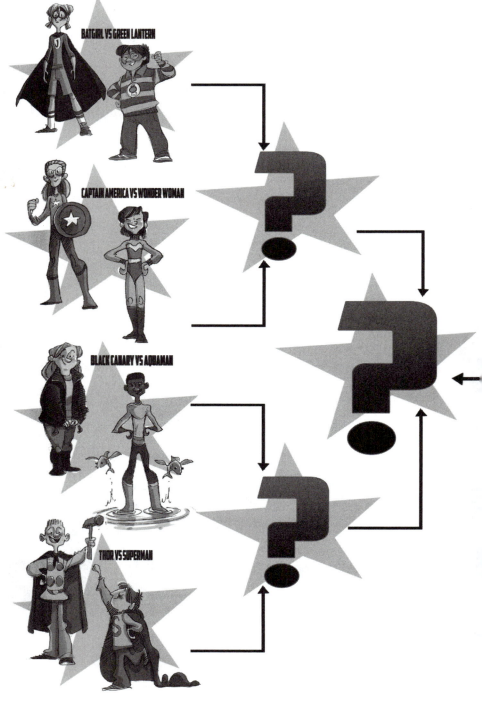

BATGIRL VS GREEN LANTERN

CAPTAIN AMERICA VS WONDER WOMAN

BLACK CANARY VS AQUAMAN

THOR VS SUPERMAN

ROUND 1

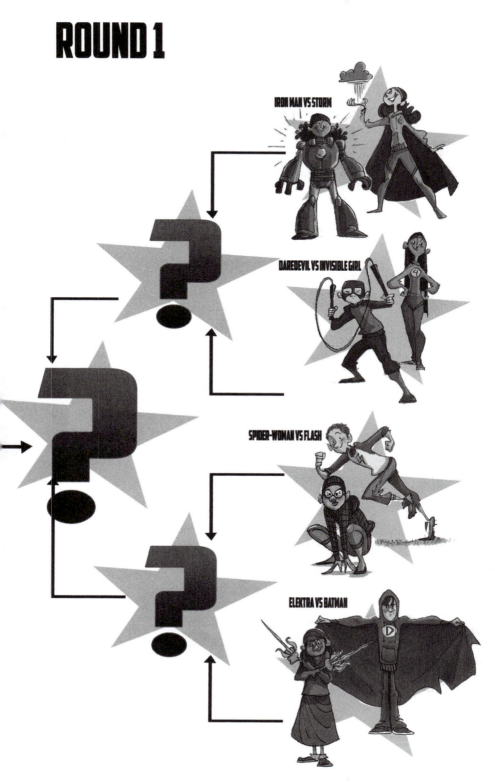

IRON MAN VS STORM

DAREDEVIL VS INVISIBLE GIRL

SPIDER-WOMAN VS FLASH

ELEKTRA VS BATMAN

THURSDAY, MARCH 12

* * Critical Thinking * * Just like Batman, all
members of the Bat-
Family need to learn
detective skills. Never really thought about it, but I
guess this links up with Batman and Batgirl having their
debuts in DETECTIVE COMICS, also known as DC! So
critical thinking and analysis are on deck!

I always have been interested in solving mysteries. I
have read a lot of Nancy Drew and I really like Sherlock
Holmes. Elementary, my dear ~~Watson~~ Jessie! Auntie G
is really into Sherlock Holmes too. She gave me THE
OFFICIAL NANCY DREW HANDBOOK for Christmas,
and there is lots of interesting stuff in there. One thing
I read today was about how to tell if somebody is lying!

I may try this out on Dylan when we get to school next
week . . .

The part I wanted to read up on was how to study body
language. Great for winning at Two Truths and a Lie.

Here are the important bits according to me . . . I used
a likely suspect — Dylan.

> How to know if Dylan is lying:
> * His eyes — if Dylan is looking around a lot,
>   blinking too much, and has big dilated pupils,
>   he might be lying.
> * If he's keeping his body really stiff but crossing
>   and uncrossing his arms and legs.
> * If he's all fidgety and nervous-looking and
>   avoiding looking me in the eye.

* If he is either really pale or really flushed.
* If he has weird breathing, like really fast or really shallow.
* If he's got a clenched jaw or tight lips or he covers his mouth with his hands . . .

You know, I think based on this list Dylan might be lying ALL THE TIME. Or none of the time. Basically he is hard to figure out. Whenever he is around me, he seems kind of on edge or freaked out or something.

More importantly, maybe Audrey should study up on this list to get better at Two Truths and a Lie. She's terrible at it. She just blurts out as much stuff as possible and then looks away, avoiding eye contact completely.

Which brings something up that I really need to think about. If I'm honest and replaced "Dylan" with "Audrey" in the list of observations above, I'd have to admit my suspicion that Audrey is hiding something from me. I trust Audrey so, so much. We've been friends forever. But I trust my gut feelings too, and more so lately. And my gut tells me something is off with my friend.

MONDAY, MARCH 16

* Critical Thinking *

It gets curiouser and curiouser every time Audrey and I try to do anything together. We used to do so much together and also text all the time.

Today I wanted to ask her about how her Iron Man exoskeleton is going. I think her idea of the superpower being used to help people who can't move their body is so good!

So I cruised up to her at the bus stop on the way home after school. I tried to chat with her, but she didn't really want to talk so I didn't push it. She said she had an assignment to work on and we went our own ways.

The problem is I couldn't help noticing that she was fidgeting with her arms (crossing and then uncrossing and crossing — it was driving me nuts). And not really looking at me. And she was kind of pale. And kind of grinding her teeth or something. What is she not telling me or who is she going off to see?

Also, even more obviously a "not truth" — what assignment did she have to work on? We don't have another assignment right now . . .

See? Curiouser and curiouser.

TUESDAY, MARCH 17

* ⭐
⭐ Critical Thinking ⭐
⭐

In class today, Mr. Richardson was talking about Sherlock Holmes and what was known about biology back in the 1900s. It was pretty neat. He talked about how the forensics and crime scene investigation Sherlock Holmes and John Watson used in the stories set in 1880 to 1914 was basically just looking at things, observing, asking questions, and being clever.

Today we have DNA samples, ballistics analysis of fired bullets, powder residue on the hand of a guy who shot a gun, not to mention fingerprints! They had nothing but their minds and magnifying glasses.

Mr. Richardson tried to make the point that we would all be awful at finding criminals if we had to do it the old-fashioned way. He said we don't pay enough attention to anything. He then went off on a bit of a rant about "hand-held devices," Facebook, Twitter, and other things "kids today" are addicted to!

But he did sort of prove his point about paying attention by leaving the room and coming back in again. He asked us if anything about him was different. Dylan, using his keen intellect, shouted out that it was later, so he was now older. Mr. Richardson just kind of stared Dylan down. When Dylan finally decided to look at his desk, he still had a bit of a smirk on his face.

Anyway, about half the class (me included) said that Mr. Richardson had changed his shirt. Great, he said, what color was it before? (It was blue now.) NO ONE could remember. It had been red. Oops.

Then he showed us this movie that some psychology guys had used in an experiment years ago. They were studying what Mr. Richardson called "inattentional blindness." Basically it means you don't notice stuff sometimes even when it's right in front of you! And they used gorilla suits to test it out!

Back in 1975, these guys at Harvard University and at Illinois University had some people pass basketballs to each other in a gym. Then they had other people watch and they asked them stuff. Like, please count how many times they pass the ball or what kind of passes they used or whatever.

Then, while people are watching all this, they had somebody dressed as a gorilla walk across the court.

Yes. An actual gorilla suit. The other guys kept passing the ball. Turns out that when the scientists asked the people (who were supposed to be watching carefully) if they saw anything unusual, about half of the people said no! This was too funny because we all noticed the gorilla-suit guy.

Mr. Richardson says this means when you pay attention to some things you don't see other things. He said that if you didn't pay attention to stuff back in the time the Sherlock Holmes stories are set, you didn't have a "redo" with video recordings or whatever. You couldn't rewind — it was just gone.

And that's when the bell rang and class ended. And then we were gone too. I actually couldn't wait to get out of there. Nobody would have noticed, but today I was doing my sense training again and I chose vision.

So here I was trying all day to pay more attention to seeing things and details of stuff. And I couldn't even remember the color of Mr. Richardson's first shirt . . . EPIC FAIL.

But it's no good just saying it's a fail without a plan to avoid failure again! I'm thinking what I need to do is try to link the things I see together into something I can remember better.

Like if Batgirl is staking out a place where bad guys are coming and going, she would try to connect the height of someone, their hat, and their car. Together that's a pattern that would be easier to remember. And to notice if it changed!

I think the key is looking for patterns.

THURSDAY, MARCH 19

* *
* Courage *
    *

It's been six months but I haven't been able to stop thinking about NYPD Sergeant Mike Bruen's experiences and courage. So I got his address from Ms. King and sent him a letter to see if he had any thoughts that I could apply to my superhero project. And today I got my reply!

Dear Mike,

Thanks so much for coming and talking to our class about your life and experiences.

I know my class already wrote a different letter to thank you, but I wanted to write and ask some more questions. It's about a school project. I hope that's okay?

Hello Jessie,

It's great to hear from you. Ms. King speaks highly of you and said I should be looking out for a message from you.

It was my pleasure to speak to your class and answer your questions—that is the best way to learn about the experiences of other people. Now, sometimes these things can be hard to talk about, but it is important to those of us who were there to pass these experiences on firsthand, so they are not forgotten.

You guys seemed genuinely interested so it was fun to me. Now let's get to your questions!

Why did you decide to be a police officer? (I can't believe NO ONE asked you this when you visited our class! I was totally going to — you may not remember but I had my hand up for a loooooong time and I NEVER put my hand up — but Ms. King said we only had time for a few questions. So, of course that included the ridiculous question from Dylan. He's the one who asked you if you ever put your lights and siren on in your squad car and drove super-fast around New York City just for fun. Dylan is a work in progress, BTW.)

Wow! Why did I become a police officer?? Hmm, let's see. I went to college to become a more "well-rounded" person (that's older adult talk for "doing lots of things") majoring in economics.

Economics was great, but I was not sure if I wanted to spend the rest of my life behind a desk. During my economic internship, I started to look around and weigh my options.

I had a cousin who was a New York Police Department officer. Even his tamest stories were extremely exciting to me. So I took the plunge and signed up as a police officer.

This became the greatest thing I could ever have done. The best description I have ever heard for my job is like having a front row seat to the greatest show on earth . . . every day.

I'm telling you it is exciting and fulfilling and always a physical and ethical challenge. You make friends for life and get to help people. Sometimes it is dangerous, of course, but it is great to be that occasional knight in shining armor.

Oh yeah. Yes. I'm guilty. I have put my lights and sirens on for no reason and drove really fast once or twice. But let's keep that our little secret, OK?

Do you have a hero you look up to?

From my mom to my dad, and the great friends I've made, and my wife and kids, I have been lucky to have many heroes. Then, as an NYPD narcotic sergeant (that means getting rid of drugs) and police officer, I have had the occasion to work beside heroes all my career. They have all affected me positively throughout my life.

Did your family worry about you when you were on duty?
Well, you know, they definitely did worry. And it would have been worse if they knew what work was really like, if I'm being honest.

But you keep most of those bad things to yourself. Only talking them through with people who have been there. My family were pretty confident that I could handle most of what was thrown at me. I always trained for the worst and hoped for the best, you know?

People (like coaches and teachers) are always talking about how we need to "conquer our fears." You've seen lots of scary stuff. Do you think people conquer fear or just get used to it?
Hmm. Do you ever defeat fears or do you just get used to them? Well, I guess a little of both. There is no substitute for training and the other side of that is there is *really* no substitute for actually doing.

Not sure if that makes sense to you, so what I mean is that you can practice doing a speech all week, but there is no substitute for getting in front of a group of people and giving your speech. Can you see what I'm getting at?

If you "own" your subject—really master it and experience it—it is easy to speak about. If you go in owning your subject, then it's easier when practice is over and the real test begins. Then after you have been tested a few times, you see you can do it.

I guess you conquer your control of your fears. They are still always there, but you can control them. You keep your wits about you and you react to the situation. The key is to stay calm. This last bit is often pretty hard to do! But you have to.

Did people in the city ever help you when you were trying to catch a bad guy?

I am happy to tell you that when the chips were down and I was in trouble, the people of New York rose to the occasion.

Once I had somebody do a subtle trip of a bad guy I was chasing, and somebody else pointed a quick finger to where the bad guy went so I could call and alert other police officers which way I was chasing someone. The people of New York helped me on many occasions.

The one I remember most was when I was by myself and a major fight ensued between me and the bad guy.

Jessie, I'll be honest. The chips were down—I was in serious trouble—and this monster was just about getting the better of me. Suddenly I heard a door unlock—you know that click sound you hear?—right in front of me. The door opens and an old grandma came out wielding a big black skillet. She smacked the bad guy over the head with that frying pan and, well, she helped me out that day. Can you believe that? I will always be in debt to her.

Do you have a favorite superhero?

Well, it has to be Batman. I believe all technology fails from time to time and as far as superheroes go, he uses technology, but Batman realizes the most important technology to winning is the super computer between your two ears. (That's your brain, get it?)

Wow. That makes me think back to what I wrote in this journal after Mike visited our class. But now I have to change my conclusion, I think. Heroes don't just run towards danger — they are ready to take action and do something about the danger when they arrive.

Do I have that kind of courage inside of me? I don't feel particularly brave a lot of the time. How do you get to be like that, I wonder? Can you learn it or does it just happen?

Maybe just by practicing the stuff I'm scared of over and over again, I'll get better.

One last thing . . . I am NOT telling Dylan that Mike Bruen likes Batman too.

FRIDAY, MARCH 20

*   *
* Courage *
   *

Today was all about fear. Or really about defeating fear. Well, that's what it was supposed to be about, anyway. But today did not exactly go as planned. Audrey and I were trying to see if I could be calm in the face of fear. You know, get scared by something but not really lose it? Just like Batgirl. And Daredevil. And Elektra and loads of superheroes.

But apparently I'm not ready for a fearsome Batgirl face-off yet. Unless it's supposed to be a face-off to reveal MY fear . . .

The idea was that Audrey should try and scare me at random times at school. The idea seemed like a pretty good one — you know, face your fears and defeat them and all that. And the general plan seemed pretty straightforward. It was supposed to go something like this.

> * Step #1. Audrey hides somewhere. Like behind a door, around a corner. Maybe even in a locker. Whatever.

167

* Step #2. I come wandering along, having completely forgotten about what Audrey was doing in step #1. This is actually easier to do than you might think. Which was part of my problem today, actually.
* Step #3. Audrey jumps out and tries to scare me, but aha! Not so fast, because . . .
* Step #4. I stay calm and carry on. You know, it's all good here people, nothing to see, move along.

Seems pretty simple. But my tendency to overreact to getting surprised made sticking to the whole plan a lot harder.

Audrey tried our plan five times today. Instead of staying calm and carrying on, I kind of freaked out instead. Which involved a lot of shouting. Shrieking might be a better description, actually. Anyway I was pretty loud. And not particularly dignified. It was a bit embarrassing. And definitely un-Batgirl-like.

More work is needed, clearly, unless my superhero plan is to confuse attackers by random hysterical behavior . . . hmmm. Maybe that should be looked at?

Anyway, while I am writing about Audrey, she and I had another friendly Batgirl versus Iron Man argument today after Socials. She has been talking about this writer Warren Ellis and what he thought about Iron Man. He wrote this Iron Man story — according to Audrey — called "Extremis."

In "Extremis," Tony Stark uses some really wild technology to basically fuse his nervous system with the armor. His suit of armor gets hooked right up to his brain. Kind of like plugging into a computer. But everywhere at once. Anyway, Audrey went on a rant about that for a while. Audrey also mentioned that another writer named Matt Fraction used a similar idea for Iron Man.

Not like Audrey thinks she can actually connect something to anyone's brain. Certainly not any of our friends or classmates. Like Dylan, as a totally random example that just popped into my head. If I was still annoyed with Dylan, I'd say that he'd need a brain in order to connect something to it in the first place. But I am more dignified than that, so I won't say it.

Audrey really likes Warren Ellis's writing and the Iron Man and X-Men comic books that he has done. She even found this session on the internet from a comic book convention. Somebody asked Warren if there was any way for Batman to beat Iron Man in a fight. He said that Iron Man "can launch munitions and fire gigawatt particle beam emissions FROM SPACE" while Batman "is dressed as a bat."

That was pretty harsh! Audrey said she's taking Ellis's answer as a no, Batman could not beat Iron Man. I said maybe the jury is still out on that. I looked up the comic book convention Audrey found and emailed writer Dennis O'Neil! He did lots of Batman and Iron Man writing and editing.

Dennis emailed back: "Obviously, Stark's technology is superior and his engineering mentality bests Bruce's. But for logic and deduction – maybe abstract reasoning – Bruce Wayne would probably win. Since both have a narrow focus, I'd nominate neither to solve the world's problems . . ."

I'm also thinking about what Mike Bruen said about how technology can fail and that's a big reason why he likes Batman. Batman uses technology, but ultimately he relies on himself.

I think it's becoming pretty clear that a great superhero needs to be good at many things. Both Hayley Wickenheiser and Clara Hughes told me that! Got to make sure I'm doing it with my own training.

SUNDAY, MARCH 29

My mom just got a call from Cade's dad! He – Cade, I mean – was in a freak snowboarding accident. He hit a tree with his head and his leg and it's broken! Got to S-L-O-W down here. His leg is broken, not his head. I'm a bit freaked out. He's such a good boarder. How could this happen? And he was wearing a helmet too! Cade's unconscious. His helmet broke when he hit the tree. And his lower leg bones are both broken!!! But the thing is he's unconscious . . . I see that I wrote that already . . . anyway. He isn't awake. He's gotta wake up!!! They said he has a concussion for sure.

I'll look it up. It'll keep me busy. I need to be too busy to cry . . . Which is pretty much all Audrey and I did on the phone a few minutes ago.

MONDAY, MARCH 30

Audrey and I went to the hospital. She is totally freaking out. We weren't allowed to go in and see Cade, but they let us look at his door. (Ugh. Too tired to erase that. We didn't look AT the door. We looked at him through the window in his door.) He looks pretty peaceful. It's like he's sleeping. But with lots of tubes in his arm and up his nose. And lots of medical machines. I tried to make a (lame) joke with Audrey that Cade looks a lot like Iron Man with all the technology connected to his body.

He's got to wake up.

He will wake up. They think so. He's in "stable condition." But not awake.

I asked Mom about what's going on. She told me a bit about concussions. But I'm too freaked to write it down now.

In order to keep from freaking out too much, Audrey spent a lot of time explaining what all the machines hooked up to Cade were doing.

> Audrey (in not really the clearest voice): "That is just the saline drip to give Cade water and drugs and stuff."

Me (not really sure what to say): "OK."

Audrey (talking very fast and kind of like a robot): "That tube in his nose is to give him oxygen. So he can breathe easier. Usually oxygen is about 20% of the air we breathe in. Cade might be getting like 95% oxygen right now, so he can breathe super easy."

Me: "Um. Right. Cool!"

Audrey (like she was going to cry again): "That little clip thingy on Cade's finger uses infrared light to check out his heart rate and how much oxygen is making its way into his blood."

Me: "That's pretty neat?"

Audrey: "That other line is for the saline drip to give Cade water and stuff . . . Did I say that already?"

Me: "Um. Yes, but no problem. You're all good."

It mostly helped. But not all the way helped. The only thing that would have helped all the way was if Cade told us to quiet down. And to do that he'd have to wake up.

TUESDAY, MARCH 31

Cade.

    Still.

        Not.

            Awake . . .

☹

Audrey and me.

    Still.

        Freaking.

            Out.

☹☹

At least Audrey and I are getting along fine, with no weirdness. Just supporting each other for our friend.

WEDNESDAY, APRIL 1

He woke up – finally! He woke up he woke up he woke up!!! ☺☺☺ Audie and I went by again after we heard. Everyone was super happy. We brought him a stack of comics to read. His favorites – Daredevil, Avengers, Batman Incorporated, and Punisher. I also slipped in the Batgirl, Birds of Prey, and Captain Marvel annuals.

Cade looked a bit confused when going through the pile of comics. I know why – he didn't see any Aquaman. But when he gets to Batgirl, he'll find Aquaman slipped inside the Batgirl cover.

I had to buy two issues of that comic, but it was worth it for this prank! Ha! Ha!

Happy April Fool's Day, Cade! ☺

FRIDAY, APRIL 3

* Recovery *

Cade is back at home now. He is doing pretty well, but he is still feeling a bit "fuzzy." He's had lots of headaches, I guess, so they want him to stay at home and kind of lay low for a bit.

Mom said that's pretty normal after a concussion. But it was still kind of strange to see him like that, being slow to answer and not having real quick comebacks when we were making fun of each other.

But considering what happened to him, I am super happy to see him doing anything.

I asked him what it was like. He said it was pretty weird. Here's a list of all the things he experienced:

* massive headache
* dizzy and poor balance
* felt sick to his stomach (and even threw up once)
* felt really down and grumpy
* has trouble remembering stuff
* sleep has been out of whack

His leg is still messed up too. And will be for a while. Apparently when he broke the bones in his lower leg, he really stretched a big nerve too. I guess they aren't supposed to stretch so much, and now he can't feel much in his foot. Just a bit of tingling.

Cade is also having some problems picking his toes up and moving his ankle. They told him it will take months before the nerve gets fixed up. Apparently it is busy regrowing. But it's super slow – growing only one millimeter each day. Yikes.

Audrey asked him if he is going to go snowboarding again when his leg is all healed up. Cade said he thinks so. So, just to encourage him, I told him the story about Shay when she fell off her horse and broke her arm.

Now, since I am the older sister, it is part of my sacred duty to make a little bit of fun of my younger sister. And kind of give her a hard time about stuff, you know? And I sort of do it, but not ALL THE TIME.

But sometimes I do it to make myself feel better, because Shay is kind of pretty awesome.

Like when she broke her arm. That wasn't so awesome.

Basically her horse went a bit haywire and took off running (if Shay were writing this, she'd use some fancy horse term like "canter" or "trot" or whatever). And then came to a sudden stop. Since there are no seat belts (who knew?) on saddles, Shay went flying off. And landed on her arm. Which snapped at her elbow.

178

Gramma was watching the whole thing. It was her first time seeing Shay ride a horse. It was also her first time seeing Shay fall off a horse. And her first time seeing Shay break her arm.

The good news is that we have some pretty funny photos of the event. Gramma took loads of pictures. So we have a bunch of Shay riding happily, Shay trotting happily, Shay waving at Gramma, Shay giggling. Just like a nice family memory. Except the last picture in the series is Shay laying on a stretcher and being loaded into an ambulance. Good times. Luckily she was fine.

I told Cade the main point I was trying to make is that Shay is doing awesome now. She's all healed up and

back riding every week. The other main point for Cade is that Shay was afraid of getting back on a horse at first. She wasn't allowed to do any riding for like three months until her bones had healed up. That entire time all she did was talk about what it would be like to ride again and couldn't she ride again now. On and on.

But when she was finally told she could ride again, she said she didn't want to. I suspect she was pretty terrified of falling again. Like, who wouldn't be, right?

Here's an excerpt from one of our conversations:

Me: "It's okay, Shay! You know what they say, get back on that horse!"

Shay: "I am terrified of falling again."

Me: "Nah, it will be fine."

Shay: "You said it would be fine last time too."

Me: "Er . . ."

Shay: "When I go riding again, I am going to leave you my hospital emergency kit."

Me: "Say what?"

Shay: "A kit with some books, my Nintendo DS, clothes, and stuff. Like for if they have to put another pin in my arm or leg. I want some stuff all packed and ready."

Me: "Don't you think you are being kinda paranoid?"

Shay: "I call it being prepared."

Me: "Well, while we're getting all prepared, if you're in the hospital for a while, mind if I use your room as a lounge? If we cut a hole in my wall, I can put a doorway straight into your room. I'll just have to move your desk and some of your junk and then . . . Hey!"

Shay sure hit hard for someone who only recently had a broken arm. She ought to watch that. All I was doing was feeling out her thoughts on some little home renovations!

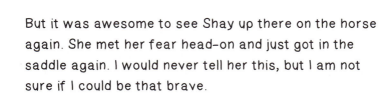

But it was awesome to see Shay up there on the horse again. She met her fear head-on and just got in the saddle again. I would never tell her this, but I am not sure if I could be that brave.

I was surprised when Cade said he wasn't sure if he could be as brave as Shay either.

MONDAY, APRIL 6

* Perseverance *

This is a MARVEL-ous diary entry! Captain Marvel, that is! Cade is feeling better and I got an answer back from Captain Marvel writer Kelly Sue DeConnick!

Dear Kelly Sue,

Wow. I am super excited to write to you. I've just read a bunch of your Captain Marvel comics — your stories are something else!

I didn't really know much about Captain Marvel at all before, actually, even though the character has been a Marvel hero since 1967. But then I learned about the science fiction bits and how Captain Marvel gets power from an alien "Kree" technology. Ricki (she works at Curious Comics where I get all my books and she's awesome) told me about how your Captain Marvel — Carol Danvers — is such an amazing female superhero! It's cool how you took Ms. Marvel and morphed her into Captain Marvel! It really made me want to ask you some stuff!

For a school project, I am trying to sort out what it would take to get the abilities of a human superhero. I settled on Batgirl. (BTW, don't get me started. It was a whole thing all on its own trying to pick one superhero to focus on.)

I'm trying to train to be a superhero, but my friend Audrey thinks a better idea is to build a superhero. Her fave is Iron Man. She's been reading Iron Man forever and was super stoked when Pepper Potts got her own suit to use.

Audrey's mom is a biomedical engineer and Audrey wants to build an exoskeleton like Iron Man. "Ambitious much?" I asked. But anyway it's a cool project. Sorry, got a little off track. Thanks for considering my questions!

Do you think it's better to become, to be, or to build a superhero?

As tempting as it is, I think it's a mistake to compare our experiences for what is "best." What's best for us is who we are. Each of our challenges is unique and we are uniquely qualified to live our lives our "best." If there's a lesson to be learned from Carol, I think that's it.

Maybe it sounds goofy, because you are writing Captain Marvel, but who is your favorite superhero? Is it different now than when you were my age? (I'm 13.)

It's not goofy! When I was 13, my favorite superhero was probably Wonder Woman. I was born in 1970 and so the Linda Carter Wonder Woman TV show got its hooks in me early.

These days it's hard to say. Probably Captain Marvel, though!

Is Captain Marvel the most powerful superhero you can imagine?

She's not, actually. But I don't really want her to be. You follow? If she were the most powerful being in the universe, it would be hard to imagine situations in which she was challenged, and Carol's challenges are the opportunities she has to learn and grow. Just like you and me, huh?

I think one of the things that makes Carol special to me is that I find her relatable. I can imagine that her thoughts, emotions, and experiences are something like my own. If she were the most powerful being in the universe . . . well, we wouldn't have very much in common then.

What does it feel like to write a girl superhero who's so amazing?
It feels pretty good.

Did you always want to write comic books? Like even when you were a teenager? Is it fun?
I didn't. When I was your age, I wanted to be an actor. My degree is actually in theater. I love my job, though. It's hard work, but it's fun and especially rewarding when I get letters from curious girls like you, Jessie.

I look forward to watching you punch holes in the sky.

Your friend,
Kelly Sue

Jessie, I just saw your P.S.!

I've just read about Amelia Earhart and her flights. Wow. She did so much way back then. Learning about her really got me into your story about the World War II squadron of women fighter pilots! It was great. My question is, why did you make your

Captain Marvel story around them?

First, I should clarify that women were not actually combat pilots in World War II—they were ferry pilots. That means that they delivered planes from one place to another so that the male pilots would be freed up for combat positions.

Did you know that women were not officially allowed into combat until 2013? It's true! History is happening all around us, Jessie.

Anyway, I chose to include the Banshee Squadon because I was thinking a lot about the idea of legacy and I wanted to remind Carol of some of the incredible women aviators who came before her.

Have you gotten around to reading about the 99ers or the Mercury 13 yet? What a bunch of wonderful discoveries you have waiting for you, Jessie. I'm jealous!

I really like how Kelly Sue describes Captain Marvel as relatable. Just like I've been doing with Batgirl. But I never thought of it quite the way she describes it: how heroes and superheroes can be so strong but still have weaknesses and fears.

But they go and do things anyway.

FRIDAY, APRIL 10

*
* Recovery *
  *
*

Mr. Richardson asked my mom to come in and talk to our class today about concussions, because she does some work with athletes who get concussions. Like football, hockey, and soccer players mostly. Mom said that the brain gets a bit damaged in a concussion, but most of the time, if treated properly, things can return to normal pretty quickly.

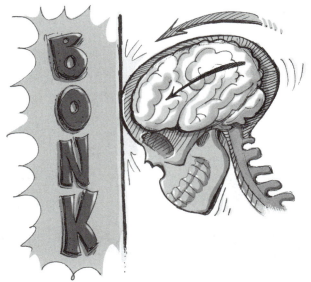

Our brain cells — those neurons — need lots of oxygen and food all the time. The more active the neurons are the more energy they need. This is my sketch of what she showed us! And my explanation of what I think she said . . .

Apparently, a big bang to the head or the body causes a big energy problem for the brain. Neurons still need lots of energy but while all this is going on, there is less blood flow getting to the neurons.

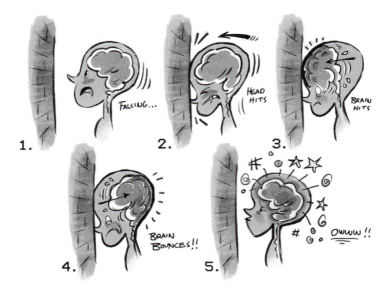

The energy is in the sugar found in the blood, so increase in hunger of those neurons at the same time that less energy is coming along means big problems. Because of that, the neurons just don't work properly for a bit and some just stop doing their jobs. They kind of "go to sleep," Mom said, and some of them don't wake up!

When the brain cells DO wake up, it's not all at once. It can take lots of neurons many days to recover! That's why it takes so long to wake up sometimes after a concussion and why there can be memory problems and confusion. It can often take weeks for things to get back to normal.

Also the chemicals that send messages between neurons — neurotransmitters — get messed up too. Returning to normal levels of neurotransmitters sometimes takes several weeks too.

I tried to think of a positive spin on this. Cade was off doing physio for his leg today so I texted to let him know he should look at his injury this way: it's actually a good thing he broke his leg. That way he couldn't go boarding right away, which would have been bad for his brain! Turns out that's why they sit out players in hockey and football after they've had a big collision.

Anyway, the most important thing is that Cade is awake again. But he won't be going boarding for a while. His next thing to try is walking.

Which reminded me of the "Batgirl Rising: Field Test" story by Bryan Q. Miller. I was just re-reading that comic (or re-re-re-reading actually — it's so good!). In "Field Test," Barbara Gordon is doing some rehab exercise with Wendy Harris. Wendy has had a spinal cord injury too (like Barbara), but she isn't coping so well. She won't take any advice or help and is basically just super angry and upset. But Barbara helps her anyway. She helps her just like a friend would.

I'm starting to see that a big part of Batgirl is how she can work together with lots of different people. Superheroes or regular people. I bet she'd even be friends with me — Superhero of Awkward — if we met in real life.

WEDNESDAY, APRIL 15

* Superhero Slam
*   Round 1 *
   *

Before we started round 1 of the Superhero Slam today, Ms. King had us review the rules of engagement. Each debate is focused on one of the Superhero Slam Great 8 qualities, drawn randomly! We each had two minutes to make our case for our superhero and then one minute to argue back against our opponent.

I was up against Green Lantern (Jack). We were both pretty nervous and then when we found out we were going to go first of all the groups, we got even more tense.

Ms. King drew out perseverance and determination, and suddenly I felt really frozen in my head and was panicking a bit. I tried to just relax. I thought about everything I've learned about facing down my fears and pushing through. About being determined. And who's more determined than me and Batgirl?

I rattled off all the descriptions of Batgirl's training with Batman, Robin, and Nightwing, how they all make her push hard and harder, how she's one of the only true heavy-hitting female superheroes, how she was inspired by her dad . . . I totally NAILED IT.

Jack looked relieved to be out of the tournament. I felt bad for him and for — well, let's be real here — totally crushing his superhero. But I also felt awesome for me. I was very scared, but I did it anyway.

After today's showdown, half the teams were eliminated. Next round, on my side of the draw it's Aquaman (Cade) versus Thor (Tim), and Batgirl (me) versus Captain America (Lillian). Yikes. On the other side, Iron Man (Audrey) takes on Invisible Girl (Amanda) and Batman (Dylan) goes up against Spider-Woman (Samantha).

If I thought beating Green Lantern would be tough (but it wasn't considering his powers don't work against YELLOW), Captain America — a war hero and icon — is going to be even more of a challenge.

But I feel different now. I rose to the challenge today. And I liked it! I'm ready for round 2.

Bring it.

SUPERHERO SLAM BRACKET

BATGIRL VS CAPTAIN AMERICA

THOR VS AQUAMAN

ROUND 2

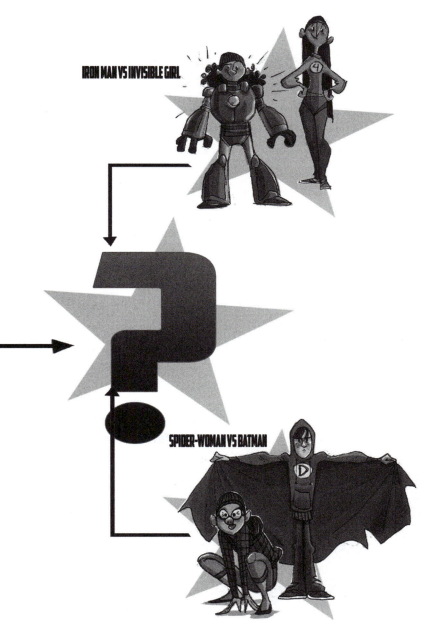

IRON MAN VS INVISIBLE GIRL

SPIDER-WOMAN VS BATMAN

FRIDAY, APRIL 24

★
★ Physical Strength
& Agility ★
★
★

Leading off with some of my need-to-knows about Batgirl's martial arts training!

* Batgirl bends like bamboo, but how can she hit a bad guy to hurt him but without doing harm?
* What would Batgirl need to do to prepare herself for defending others?
* As a smaller fighter, what kind of skills would she need so she can avoid opponents while defeating them by evasion and counter-attacking?

In the comics, one of the best Batgirl fighters is Cassandra Cain. The Cassandra Cain Batgirl is actually the 17-year-old daughter of David Cain, one of the martial arts teachers of Bruce Wayne (a.k.a. Batman!). So, let's just say she has a solid background.

I've been doing karate with Auntie G, but if I was really, really for real and true trying to be Batgirl, what other types of martial arts would I need to study?

To be honest, until I started doing it myself, I used to think of martial arts as a guy thing. Which is a weird idea for me to have, when I think about it, especially with Auntie G being so martial artsy. But there it is.

Funny, it turns out martial arts

training is about making weaker into strong, not just strong into stronger. Auntie G says judo is like that as well, and some other martial arts too. Also, there are some martial arts really well suited to small and quick people (like me and Batgirl).

Auntie G told me to look up a kind of Shaolin kung fu known as Wing Chun. Wing Chun was supposedly created by a young woman named Yim (yes, the next bit is kind of predictable) Wing Chun.

Turns out the Chinese symbols for Wing Chun literally mean "forever springtime." Which is kind of poetic when you think about it. Gramma would've loved it. She loved all kinds of neat stuff. Comic books, the old serial movies they used to show before movies. She sure loved movies. She also thought Tarzan was a super-hero. Which at first made me laugh! I didn't really think of Tarzan as a superhero. But Gramma explained that she liked how athletic he was and could swim and climb and was very powerful. She liked reading about him in the comics and seeing Tarzan movies when she was young. And now I kind of get it. Lots of physical ability, just like Batgirl.

Wing Chun techniques are about training for the best body shape and form. You are supposed to be like a piece of bamboo and "bend but not break" (Auntie G's words for me too!). Wing Chun is the martial art that Bruce Lee studied originally.

Be firm but flexible, be strong and rooted, but also yielding. Auntie G praised judo for this too. I think I should learn more about judo, actually!

This is very important for Batgirl — and girls in general — who may have to fight against much larger opponents. It's all about deflecting and redirecting.

Seems to me that an important idea here is to use tools — like the karate stick — to help make things more equal. I've been doing karate stick (Auntie G calls it a staff; the real word in Japanese is "bo"), and it's harder than punching and kicking.

Auntie G said to check out some other women who were great martial artists. Like Keiko Fukuda, 10th degree black belt and the highest ranked woman in judo.

Keiko Fukuda has an amazing story! She lived to be 99 years old and was super active her whole life. It turns out there's a documentary about her life called MRS. JUDO playing at a theater in town! I am going to ask if Ms. King would consider a class trip to see an educational movie like that!

The director of the movie is a woman named Yuriko Romer. She actually lives on the West Coast just like me.

Guess who's getting a letter!

MONDAY, APRIL 27

How's this for weird? I just tried getting a hold of Audrey but she wasn't answering her email or her phone (or texts). So I called her house and her mom said she'd gone over to the rehab center with Cade to help with his physiotherapy for his leg.

Which is totally fine. Except it's not like Audrey's a physiotherapist! Why didn't he ask me to help out too? Just because Audrey's on the swim team and I'm not?

Curiouser and curiouser . . . or insulting even? I know Dylan thinks I'm nothing but a sidekick, but do my friends think that too?

I wanted to talk to Audrey about the Superhero Slam. I'm freaking out a bit about it. I guess I'm on my own with it for now . . .

THURSDAY, APRIL 30

* Perseverance *

Today in Socials, I brought up the idea of the whole class seeing MRS. JUDO. I told her how much I loved it and Ms. King was totally excited by it too. It looks like we may do it as a class trip! Hooray! Which made getting a letter back from Yuriko Romer — judo moviemaker — even more exciting!

197

Dear Yuriko,

I have to admit I don't know much about judo, actually. I started doing karate this year with my aunt. It's super fun but hard too. Auntie G is my martial arts teacher (she does karate and Okinawan weapons). She read about you and the movie you directed, MRS. JUDO: BE STRONG, BE GENTLE, BE BEAUTIFUL.

She thinks said Keiko Fukuda Sensei was a great role model for girls who want to do just about anything. Auntie G also said you were a great role model for making your movie!

For a school project, I am trying to sort out what it would take to get the abilities of a human super-hero. I am not trying to actually be a superhero and fight crime or anything! But I am trying to find out how much training would really be needed to do stuff like that.

I really hoped I could ask you some questions — I want to be a journalist — about you and Keiko Fuku-da. Then when I watched your movie, I was just like blown away. That was crazy that Fukuda Sensei's grandfather was one of Jigoro Kano's teachers! And that when Kano Sensei made judo he invited Fukuda to come and train in the women's section.

By the way, I have to tell you that a lot of girls that were at the movie (including me) started gig-gling when we got to the part when Fukuda Sensei says her mom wanted Kano Sensei to find her a husband. Her mom wanted her in judo to get her married! Yikes.

Do you know why there was originally a separate women's judo section?

Long ago when they started teaching judo to women, it was radical and new. I think they wanted to have a special separate space just for women to feel comfortable and safe, and maybe for the men to preserve their own space. Fukuda Sensei began judo in 1934, at a time when women never showed their legs and walked very daintily. So to have them dressed in judo uniforms and making aggressive physical movements was very unusual. If you look closely at some of the very old photos and film in the movie, you'll see that they used to bind up the bottoms of the pant legs. I think this was for modesty. I also think that in those days women and men were often separated for a lot of things. It all seems crazy now, but we live in a very different time.

Do you know why women had only five black-belt levels but men had 10? Isn't that kind of weird?

It seems very unfair to us now. Originally women did not compete in the Olympic-style fighting competition of judo. Women have only been competing since the 1960s; it was only 1988 when they admitted women's judo to the Olympics. I suppose that the men who were making the rules thought that without the competition aspect, five degrees of black belt would be plenty. Of course now it seems crazy to think that men and women had different standards. But then some would point out that there are still places in today's society where men and women are not paid equal salaries for professional positions or given equal opportunities. Yes, it is weird, and hopefully things keep changing so that one day equality regarding ranks, opportunities, salaries etc. will be a non-issue.

I really like in the movie when Fukuda Sensei said, "It's more important to be a good human being . . . to help other people." (Or something like that — I'm close I think!) Did she say stuff like that a lot?
Yes, Fukuda Sensei said stuff like that all the time, and she meant it. She wanted people to understand that judo was about a lot more than throws, armbars, and choke-holds. She saw judo as life. I spent a lot of time with Fukuda Sensei, but not being a judo person, I always heard her wisdom and philosophy pertaining to life. She was the most hard-working, forgiving, and under-standing person I know. There were many times when I thought, "How can I finish this movie? It is just too hard!" But then I would look to Fukuda Sensei and think of her words, and I found the strength to keep going. I still think of her and it makes me think about being a good human being, even when I don't want to be.

How did you meet Fukuda Sensei? What made you want to make a movie about her? Did you ever study judo with her?
I read an article about Fukuda Sensei in Oprah Win-frey's *O* magazine. When I realized that her dojo was in my neighborhood in San Francisco, I went to meet her. She was happy to be able to talk to me in Japanese, so she invited me to her house for tea. After hearing about her life, I realized I should make the documentary film about her. Like you, I was doing karate at the time. I

thought about learning judo, but I think it was the right thing to concentrate on the filmmaking.

Do you have a favorite superhero?

I think you are too young to know of *The Avengers*, but when I was your age I wanted to be Emma Peel, the woman agent of a British spy TV show. She was a secret agent; she was the best. I also liked Wonder Woman, because she was one of the only woman superheroes around. Today I look around and I see many real female superheroes! I hope we keep adding more and more women to our list of superheroes.

Wow. When Auntie G said that Fukuda Sensei was a great role model, she really nailed it. That must've been so hard to do what she did when she did it. No other women were doing what she wanted to do. But she did it because she wanted to and thought it was right.

And her saying of "Be strong, be gentle, be beautiful"? How awesome. I want to use that too. I am so glad that Yuriko Romer wrote back to me.

Inspiration for perspiration? I can hardly wait to see Auntie G again and train with her!

FRIDAY, MAY 8

* * * Physical Strength * * Wicked! Auntie G showed me how to break boards tonight. OK. Not "boards" plural but "a board." But still, I got my Karate Kid on all right. Totally crazy . . . she broke a stack of five boards with one giant sword hand chop! It was

awesome. I used a hammerfist to break the board. For someone my size and level of training, a hammerfist or a palm heel is safest. When I am a fifth-degree black belt, I can try whatever technique I want!

Later I asked Dad why I could break a board without it breaking my bones. Makes sense, right? Dad said bones are way stronger than stuff like wood and even bricks and concrete. It's because bones are squishy! My bones have all kinds of little tiny tubes filled with water. So hitting stuff with my hand means my hand can take a lot of the energy by squishing. Bending but not breaking, I guess.

He showed me a YouTube video about this idea that squishy stuff stays in one piece and inflexible stuff breaks. This guy is shown in super slo-mo hitting a rubber ball. It's squishy like crazy and zooms off the racket. Next they take the same ball and dunk it in liquid nitrogen. Which mega freezes the ball. When the racket hits it this time, the ball breaks into a billion pieces!

That idea of bend but don't break is for real!

I guess this is another one of the things I've learned this year that I could never have imagined possible before. Who is Jessie? I am not sure anymore. But I'm definitely more bendy, which hopefully means I can't be broken!

MONDAY, MAY 11

In case she's lurking around here somewhere, I'll say
that today I went to watch Shay's horse lesson. Or, her
"riding lesson" I guess is what she calls it.

In case Shay's not lurking around here somewhere, I
should say I was forced to go watch her lesson. You
know how it is.

Apparently Mom and Dad only have so much time
to drive both of us to stuff. (Who knew?) And that
means Shay and I have to go to each other's activities
sometimes. Lame. But what are you going to do?

Anyway, I watched her get the horse from the stable,
put the gear on (which Shay corrects to "tack up"), and
then work on her skills. She has a competition coming
up and she's running through a bunch of stuff.

I'd like to keep being dismissive here, but she's actually
pretty good! Wow. I remember when she started riding
and could hardly do anything. I guess I haven't been
paying attention because she is, like, trotting and
cantering (riding faster?) and all kinds of jazz now.

I'm not the only one getting better at something!

But that wasn't the most surprising thing. The most surprising thing was Shay asked me how I was doing with the Superhero Slam. She even offered to do a pretend debate with me later if it would help!

Apparently if you give them a chance, there are lots of people trying to help out!

TUESDAY, MAY 12

* ★ Critical Thinking ★ * Something that doesn't make a lot of sense to me is this — how does Batgirl keep from getting injured all the time? What is the difference between good (keep working through it) pain and bad (stop right now) pain during exercise?

Auntie G was trying to get me to remember this little poem. It went something like this:

206

Hurt rather than harm,
Harm rather than injure,
Injure rather than kill,
Kill rather than be killed.

Which made me think of two things. "Hurt rather than harm" means there's a difference between hurt and harm. Avoiding both hurt and harm would be best! But harm is lasting whereas hurt can just be quick — like a warning — and then gone without lasting damage.

Sometimes when we are training, I bonk my arm or whatever and it hurts. So I used to stop. Then Auntie G told me, "Suck it up, princess. You're going to be OK, and you gotta keep fighting! The bad guys aren't going to give up if you get an owie!" At first I thought she was kinda harsh.

But we sat down and talked about it later. It makes sense. It's kind of like when I used to ditch it in the middle of an axel during skating. It hurt my bum landing on the ice but I really didn't have any harm come to me. Like I didn't break anything.

So it's get back up and go again!

But then there's the pain of injuries. Like when I pulled a muscle trying to kick a soccer ball last fall. All I was doing was running along and then kicking. But it felt kind of funny in the back of my leg and it hurt when I walked. (Hitting the actual ball would probably have been helpful . . .)

I remember hearing my uncle say once, "I threw my back out just lifting up a jug of milk at breakfast time." That seemed kind of lame. But my simple run wasn't a big event either, but I ended up with a real leg injury.

I did some research and found out that's because my muscles (and other stuff in my body) are just like lots of other materials. Every time I use them, I strain them and repetitive stress can weaken them. However, my body is constantly rebuilding itself.

Despite that, small little things can really be the proverbial "straw that broke the camel's back." Batgirl is constantly straining her body at the best of times and getting really pummeled at the worst of times. She has to have strength and courage just to pick herself up and keep training all the time.

How much can I really do? I still don't know the answer, or if there even is a real answer. My answer so far is I can do a whole lot more than I thought I could.

Which maybe means I sometimes try to do too much. I need to be smart about how much I can do, and sometimes pushing too hard is just . . . pushing too hard. Time for a bit of a break!

Now, where are my comics?

WEDNESDAY, MAY 20

*
* Superhero Slam *
   * Round 2 *

Superhero Slam round 2 today and, well, it was surprisingly not that difficult to beat Captain America. Sorry, Lillian! She did her best but I have to say that getting "recovery" as our attribute to debate helped me lots.

We both made some good arguments about how hard it is to get where we need to be as superheroes. I had the slight edge because as Batgirl I needed more training. Captain America had a special super-soldier serum treatment to help him.

But what really kicked me over the top was the rebuttal round. Lillian said her superhero was frozen in ice for, like, 60 years and then thawed to be Captain America in the 21st century. It's crazy hard to live in a world where all your friends are way old or dead. Plus after not moving around for so long he would have been so weak. He had to retrain himself and recover his Captain America powers!

She made a pretty good point, I have to admit.

But I didn't say that during the debate, of course.

Instead, I pulled out all the stops and laid down my story about Batgirl getting hurt really badly when Joker shot her and ripped up her spinal cord. She was in a wheelchair after that. But she still trained herself to be in great shape.

More importantly she used her other skills — her computer smarts and detective abilities — to work in the Bat-Family team as Oracle. She created a new version of Batgirl that, I argued, contributed even more than she had when she was physically on the streets fighting crime. So she still helped save everyone, but in a different way.

On the friend front, Audrey squeaked past Invisible Girl (they debated "courage") and Dylan as Batman just crushed Spider-Woman. I can't believe he got to debate "experience." He has the superhero that's probably the most experienced of any hero anywhere. He was totally lucky.

Of course, since he beat a female superhero, he went on another rant about how boys were better than girls. He is up against Audrey as Iron Man in the semi-finals. Go, Audrey, go! All the girls are behind you!

What was pretty funny was how Cade managed to out-debate and beat Thor! They both made some really good points, but they were debating "leadership." Cade did really well talking about protecting the sea and fighting for the weak and helping all the marine life to work together. He explained how Aquaman worked with all the sea creatures from the smallest krill all the way up to the great blue whale, and he would get them to work together to overcome problems. He led by example. By doing it himself.

Poor Thor didn't have much more than "My father is Odin, king of the Norse gods." And only Thor can lift the mighty hammer MJOLNIR. Basically he was saying, "I am the strongest and I will lead everyone." He didn't really talk about any kind of leadership at all.

That means for the semi-finals it's me versus Cade and Audrey versus Dylan. What a showdown.

But I'm still buzzing about beating Captain America. BAM! KAPOW! I'm rocking this Superhero Slam. I think I might be able to, you know, actually win. For somebody who's always been too shy to speak up, it turns out I'm pretty good at thinking on my feet and talking in front of people!

At least I'm not (as) terrified anymore. Maybe the Batgirl in me is showing herself?

SATURDAY, MAY 23

* Preparation *

It's funny how sometimes you think you know all about something but then it turns out you don't, not really.

For the longest time I just thought all the movements and routines in karate were for exercise. Well, they are. But what I mean is ONLY for exercise. The patterns — or "kata" — that Auntie G has been showing us are full of fighting moves.

Auntie G says that the old karate masters put together their favorite moves into packages you could remember

and practice. I've been working on one called Pinan Nidan. It has some really cool moves in it. And an interesting idea.

The idea is that if you learn some special fighting skills, you should be careful using them with others. And if you get good enough, you should try to hurt someone before trying to harm them.

Auntie G explained how our bodies have lots of sensors in them. In our skin, muscles, and all over the place. Some of them are for telling us if we are going to be hurt.

But BEFORE we actually get hurt, some of our body sensors warn us we will get hurt if we don't stop what we are doing. Reminded me of times in soccer when I've been kicked and tripped and fell down. It felt like I was injured but really I was fine.

Auntie G said we can use this response when people try to do bad things. (Auntie G ALWAYS makes it clear

we only fight against baddies.) Making them feel some pain works on the sensors to make them stop what they are doing. Like in a Batgirl comic book when she grabs a bad guy's arm and pushes hard on — or hits — a nerve at the elbow. It hurts so much that he stops, but it doesn't really harm him. If he comes back again, she does have to harm him.

Auntie G's other motto tonight was "hope for the best, prepare for the worst." Yep, that doesn't sound that super happy, but it sounds realistic! I think Mike Bruen would definitely agree with Auntie G.

WEDNESDAY, MAY 27

*
★ Superhero Slam ★
★ Semi-Final ★

I'm super happy . . . but I'm kind of sad too. I feel pretty mixed up, actually.

Today in the Superhero Slam I beat Cade. I made it to the finals but I'm feeling down.

I was so freaked out before our debate. Freaked out because Cade is one of my best friends and I didn't want to beat my friend. But also freaked out because I want to win the Superhero Slam and Cade has been awesome in it. I knew he would be hard to beat. So I was kind of scared/freaked out.

I was so nervous I was actually shaking a bit before Ms. King drew out the attribute. I could not believe it when she pulled out "preparation." That's like one of the best possible ones for Batgirl — she's all about training and research and always improving. But it's one of the all-time worst ones that could ever be chosen for Aquaman. He just . . . goes and does stuff with water.

And Cade knew it. Poor Cade! His face actually dropped when she read out "preparation." He may have actually said a swear word (or two, actually) under his breath.

Aquaman is all about natural talent, not preparation. Cade did his best, but he didn't have much to work with. And I had lots to work with. It wasn't pretty at all. I crushed a great pal.

Anyway, a pretty big day! I'm pretty excited that I won, actually, but also sad that to win I had to beat my friend. I don't even want to write about it because it's kind of upsetting, but Audrey lost to Dylan — Batman beat Iron Man! It's just not as fun when I have some weirdness with my friends and now both Audrey and Cade are out of the Slam.

Is it okay that I like being successful in this tournament even if it means beating my friends? And is this going to affect my friendship with Cade?

TUESDAY, JUNE 2

This entry is out of this world! I love getting mail, especially when it's an answer to one of my letters. Here's my interview of Nicole Stott — NASA astronaut and engineer! She's spent over 103 days in space including her time on the International Space Station and the Space Shuttle.

Dear Nicole,

As part of a big school project, I'm looking at how or if a girl could train to Batgirl's skill level. Anyway, we were talking about stress and life in biology and I was thinking about how stress relates to Batgirl.

My science teacher, Mr. Richardson, suggested I write to you. I researched you and found out lots of cool things about you! Like how on October 21, 2009, you did the first live tweet from space during your Expedition 21 mission with NASA. Sweet! And how you have been in space on six different missions including living on the International Space Station for three months.

I have a bunch of questions for you. I hope you can answer some of them for me.

How much did you pack to go to the Space Station? Was it hard to figure out what to take with you?
This may sound hard to believe, Jessie, but for a three-month trip to the space station I took one pair of pants, one sweater, a couple of t-shirts, some shorts, some work-out clothes, and a few other items. Not very much. My guess is your eyes have just gone kind of glassy thinking about this! You are no doubt wondering how we keep our clothes clean enough to get by with that pretty small number of items for three months. And no, we don't have a washing machine or a dryer on the space station. The trick is your clothes don't get that dirty and not in the same way they do on Earth. That means you can pack pretty light.

On Earth with normal gravity, your clothes kind of

lay against your body most of the time. So your clothing is picking up all the oils and so on that you have on your body. But in space your clothes more sort of float around you and don't stick to you in the same way. They stay cleaner and useful a lot longer.

What was the first thing you did in space?
Well, it may not sound too exciting, but basically the first thing I did was get to work! Depending on where you are sitting on the way to orbit you can have a pretty good view out the window of space and Earth—which is awesome! We also had special wrist bands with mirrors so we could see around us. But once you get to the station, there's lots to do. And that's totally fine. That's why I wanted to get up there in the first place!

What did you do in your free time on the space station? Do you have any hobbies you can do in space?
We are pretty busy when we are up there and working a lot. But I like photography and I was fascinated by watching everything unfold beneath me. Looking for different landmarks on Earth—like, "Hey, there's Florida again"—and seeing things at different times of day. It was amazing and constantly changing and I really loved taking pictures of it. And also trying to do some watercolors!

I brought some paints with me that I used with a very special brush. A dear friend of mine—who's an outstanding artist—gave me a paintbrush to bring up in orbit with me. It was given to him by his teacher and it was the first one he ever had! So it was pretty neat to bring that up to the International Space Station and paint with it.

You're probably wondering how you paint in microgravity? Very carefully. Actually, it's pretty much like painting on Earth but you just have to try and be a bit more careful to not get paint everywhere and make a mess.

While I was painting or taking pictures (and lots of other astronauts take many photographs too), some of my friends were playing music. There's a keyboard up there and one of my friends Cady Coleman brought up a flute to play. On an upcoming mission Karen Nyberg is going to do some quilting!

How does it feel when you first get back to Earth? Is it harder getting used to being in orbit or getting used to Earth again?

It feels good to be back on Earth again and closer to family. That's what I missed the most—my family. But it also felt super heavy. I mean that literally. Like my body felt heavier than I could ever have imagined. I remember coming back and it felt like the lower part of my leg weighed, like, 100 pounds.

They do all kinds of tests and so on before and after a mission. On this one return, they had laid out these small orange safety cones. Like the ones you see on the road, you know? Except these were only about four-inches tall, really tiny ones, almost like baby safety cones. And they wanted us to jump over them. No problem, right? You could easily jump four-inches high I bet! Well, looking at those cones it was so hard to imagine being able to make my body do it and ever get my body to jump that high. And when I did it, it felt really funny.

Lots of stuff you normally don't pay any attention

to—like just keeping your head up when you stand and move—took all kinds of extra thinking just to get it happening. It was like my neck forgot its job of holding my head up!

Of course, I was able to do it once I kept practicing. That's the thing that I find really amazing. Both for going into space and microgravity and coming back to Earth and regular gravity. My brain figured it out pretty fast. Just like how I adapted to space, I was able to adapt to normal gravity. Probably it's easier to adjust to orbit because you're so psyched to be up in space. It kind of overrides the awkwardness.

But I do remember coming back from one mission. I was lying down the whole way back because I had been in space for over three months. Once we were back on the runway, I had to kind of roll off the recumbent chair/bed I was on and crawl over to the hatch to get out. There I was, crawling along on my hands and knees to get out that hatch. I remember thinking I had to do the heaviest squat lift I had ever done in my life just to lift up my own body to get out. Somehow I did it and was up and walking and feeling *very* heavy.

What do you miss about space when you are back on Earth?

Well, in addition to the fantastic view of the Earth, I really missed the graceful feeling of floating and moving around. At first when I got to space, I felt kind of clunky and awkward. It was hard to coordinate my body to float around. But pretty quickly my brain figured out how to help me do things and my awkwardness became a kind of graceful movement.

It's kind of interesting. We think we live on Earth in three dimensions. You know, length, height, width. And we do. But you really don't understand the idea of volume of a room until you are in microgravity and you can float around and use the whole room. Maybe you've experienced something similar if you've ever gone snorkeling or scuba diving?

When you are at the surface of the water, it's like when we are in a room here on Earth. You move along side to side but not so much up and down. Then if you dive to the bottom to see a shell or a coral reef or something, you are using the 3-D idea and exploring the volume of the water. In space it's just like that—except you don't have to hold your breath.

I also really miss the friendships with my crewmates. And the whole sense of the amazing adventure that you are part of when you are up there.

What was the most dangerous thing you experienced in space?

Luckily we didn't have any major dangerous things happen during my six missions in space. But we always, always train, train, and train and prepare in case something happens. Because the truth is the whole idea of going outside Earth's atmosphere into space is all dangerous! If you think about, even launching could be pretty dangerous. You are taking off from Earth on a huge rocket that has to be powerful enough to escape our gravity. Lots of what is going on is out of your control.

Like I said, though, we did so much training so we could respond to things we could control if something did happen. Like on a spacewalk or if there is a problem on the station or whatever spacecraft you are on.

There are three main things we always had to be ready to deal with:

1) A hole in the spacecraft. This could be very bad because you could lose all the pressurization and the atmosphere you need to live up in orbit.

2) Fire. Fire is a problem wherever you are, but up on the Space Station it's a huge concern. Even if you get a fire put out, the problem with smoke is still there. It's not like at home where you can just open up the windows and air out the house!

3) Toxic spill. Now, we don't have a lot of what you might think of as huge toxic worries. Like radioactive waste! Instead our main worry is ammonia. It's in our coolant system and if there was a leak it could be a real problem because it would poison us.

And we did have a number of alarms that would go off. They all turned out to be false alarms. But of course you only know they are false alarms *after* you have done everything you need to do if the problem really was there. To be honest, though, having some false alarms and seeing how well we all performed our duties (because we trained so much) made me feel comfortable that we would be okay no matter what.

How much exercise do you get? Do you feel gross from not moving so much?

Actually I did two hours of workout exercise each day—which is way more than I have time to do when I'm on Earth. We have to do so much because you lose so much bone and muscle strength really fast in space.

We did cardio and strength exercise. The cardio "aerobic" exercise was on a really neat treadmill and cycle ergometer that had straps and harnesses so you could stay on them and not go flying off! You don't notice it so much I bet, Jessie, but when you push down on your bike pedal, it pushes back. In space there's not enough gravity working on your body to hold you down so you need straps instead. And we also had special exercise devices for doing strength training.

The funny thing is you move around way more in space than you do on Earth. But it's in microgravity so it isn't so tiring.

How do you have a shower in space?

You don't really have a shower in space. That would be pretty messy and use lots of water. Instead you have a kind of sponge bath. But because water kind of hangs together in a blob, it's pretty weird. You kind of make a big globe of water that you push parts of your body through. Then the water just kind of coats your body, you add some soap, coat it again, and clean up. It's pretty wild. It made washing my long hair a lot more work too! But I got used to it.

Of course, when you sweat while exercising the same thing happens. Your body kind of gets slicked up with sweat. So you have to constantly use a towel to dry off. I never realized how much my scalp sweats until being in space!

Have you ever heard of the 99s?

Well, Jessie, yes I have! I am a member of the 99s, actually. The full name is the Ninety-Nines: International

Organization of Women Pilots. It's a really neat group for sharing experiences and excitement with other women. About spreading the word about what's possible for everyone. And maybe inspire some girls or women to try something they might not otherwise think they could do.

Do you have a favorite superhero?
I don't really have a favorite superhero as such. But I have come across—or learned about—some really inspirational people. Like Beryl Markham. She was the first woman to fly across the Atlantic Ocean from east to west. She did it all by herself way back in 1936. She wrote a kind of diary-style book about her life and I came across it a few years ago. It is called *West with the Night* and it's so inspirational. Beryl was a real pioneer and has inspired me ever since.

I think it's so cool to read about an inspiring woman like Nicole and then learn about who inspired HER! And finding out about how hard being in space is. The idea of forgetting how to use my body is blowing my mind! It's like the total opposite of doing all this Batgirl training to learn how to use my body better.

But probably the most important thing I could learn from Nicole is how to be prepared. Being in space means having to think of EVERYTHING in advance. There's no way to change what you brought with you or what's on the space station once you're up there.

That includes you! When she writes, "We always train, train, train and prepare in case something happens," it sounds like something Auntie G would say about training martial arts with me! Batgirl – think ahead! Prepare for the hardest and hope for the best! With all the training you can actually just react to what's happening and get the job done.

I hope . . .

WEDNESDAY, JUNE 10

A few weeks ago I started an entry like this: "It's funny how sometimes you think you know all about something but then it turns out you don't, not really."

Well, it applies here too. Even though everything was hours ago, I'm actually still getting a little worked up while I write this!

At lunch, things were great. Audrey was extra friendly and offered her dessert to me. I love tapioca pudding!

Then Cade came over just as lunch break was finishing. Right before the bell, actually. He had great timing! He said he was sorry about how everything had gone lately with Audrey and me and wanted to make it up to me after school. Could I meet them by my locker?

I said sure I guess. I'd be there anyway getting ready to go. So there's no law saying they couldn't come by too. But I did wonder why Cade was apologizing for problems between me and Audrey. What's he got to do with it?

Clearly something was up. And I was freaking about it all afternoon. Was Cade actually upset about losing to me in the Superhero Slam? Was he angry at me? Had he and Audrey been complaining about me when I wasn't around?

So even though I was still worried, I was relieved by the time the dismissal bell rang — soon I'd know what was up.

There I was grabbing my stuff when Cade and Audrey came by. Actually, they were acting super creepy! I was standing facing my locker when Cade came up from my right and Audrey mysteriously appeared on my left. Cade had his right arm kind of leaning up against the locker next to me and had his other hand behind his back (semi-spoiler alert: this is an important part of the story).

Cade started talking to me about how awesome my debate against him was! What? And how he was totally pulling for me to beat Dylan. And how Audrey and he were both going to help me get ready to beat Dylan. And how such great friends shouldn't be acting like we were lately. Then Audrey tapped me on the shoulder and complimented my outfit. While I was looking fabulous today, it must be said, because of the distance between us lately, I wasn't sure how to respond.

Then I saw her look over my shoulder and nod. My Spidey sense was tingling and I just suddenly dodged off to the right and past Cade.

Just like doing karate with Auntie G — I got out of the way. I wasn't sure what I was getting out of the way from, but there it was.

It turns out I was getting out of the way of Cade handing me a box of chocolates and a card with three tickets (plus popcorn included) to the new superhero movie coming out this weekend.

I was stunned. Then Audrey said she likes Cade and he likes her. Like, like-likes. And I said that's great but why did that affect us? Audrey said she thought I was crushing on Cade too and was jealous . . .

I just started laughing.

I told them I thought Cade was upset because I (Batgirl) had beaten him (Aquaman) SO BADLY in the Superhero

227

Slam! And that they didn't like me anymore because I wasn't on the swim team.

But now we are all on the same page again.

I'm SO relieved!

THURSDAY, JUNE 11

* Superhero Slam *

Well, just another Thursday in the last month of school for grade 8. Except now that everything is good with Cade, Audrey and me, I can finally celebrate my win!

I MADE THE FINALS! I MADE THE FINALS!

Aaaaand it's Batgirl versus Batman.

Girl versus Boy . . .

Jessie versus Dylan . . .

Holy tension, Batman!

FRIDAY, JUNE 19

Can Batgirl really beat Batman? That's the question that's been on my mind since it's come down to Dylan and me in the final of the Superhero Slam. But it was Cade who actually asked it today. He didn't say it in a bad way, you know, like Dylan would have. Like (in awful Dylan voice): "Can lame Batgirl beat Batman? NO!"

Instead Cade just came out and asked. He said he's been thinking over that conversation Dylan and Audrey had back in the fall about men and women, now that Dylan and I are pitted against each other. That argument ended in a shouting match (and a bit of learning about tennis), but this one is a real debate.

Audrey and Cade want to help get me prepared to do my best.

I'm freaking out, actually.

Has it really come down to Batgirl versus Batman?!

Calm down, Jessie!!!

Stop shouting at yourself!!!

When I look back at the list of possible debate topics, there's really only one I'm worried about: critical thinking. I know I'm good at analysis and Batgirl is amazing. But that's one place where Batman is THE king. He's the absolute best. There's no way I can beat Batman if Ms. King draws "critical thinking."

Audrey and Cade went through all the scenarios with me for the other seven attributes. I've already done courage, experience, and perseverance.

My tummy is all upside down and I know I'm going to have a tough time sleeping tonight. And probably every night until the Slam.

It all goes down next week.

No matter what, it will all be over by next Wednesday.

SATURDAY, JUNE 20

* ★
★ Critical Thinking *
★

Auntie G could tell I was
thinking too much about
stuff while I was supposed
to be training with her. I told her all the freaking out I'm
doing in my head about the final of the Superhero Slam
and going up against Dylan as Batman.

Auntie G said Batgirl has to be able to "use her body
effectively." She also has to be able to do so while
using techno-stuff. She has loads of tools, really, when
you get right down to it.

Using her body effectively means hitting with her whole
body . . . and when Auntie G hits the punching bag, that
punching bag knows it got hit. And got hit HARD. It's
pretty amazing.

Batgirl also uses actual tools as weapons when fighting
legions of evil losers. Even if those weapons are as
simple as a stick or a batarang. They even the score
and put her on a level footing with larger attackers.

Auntie G has been teaching me to see things in a room
that I could use to defend myself . . . including the
room itself. A lot of Batgirl's training is about how to
incorporate her tools and technology with her body.

Learning and remembering motor skills with tools and
tech can be even more difficult than without tools. This
is also why learning to play something like field hockey
or golf is so difficult.

When I do karate stick training, I know that my stick isn't actually part of my body, but I hope that eventually it will "become part of my body" if it is going to be really useful.

Auntie G then said something that really made me think: Batgirl works with and uses everything and everyone. She uses physical tools, like a stick or a batarang, but has to understand how they work in order for them be useful for her. Same with her friends. She needs to know their strengths and weaknesses and how they match up with hers in order to be so successful.

She applies all her training to everything she does. She IS her training. Which sounds a lot like what Nicole Stott was saying.

> Auntie G: "OK Jess, I'm going to lay some sayings on you here. 'The true science of martial arts means practicing them in such a way that they will be useful at any time, and to teach them in such a way that they will be useful in all things.' That was written by a famous sword master in old Japan named Miyamoto Musashi. He died back in 1645."

> Me: "So, you're saying my training can be useful for other things besides the actual training?"

> Auntie G: "Yes! Good one, kiddo! I think I've got an idea that will help you with the Superhero Slam. But I want you thinking the right way before I explain. So we'll get there with one more

martial arts quote. My teacher used to say this one a lot. 'The pen and the sword are one.' What do you think that means?"

Me (honestly feeling confused so I tried for a weak joke): "Try not to cut yourself when you're doing your homework?"

Auntie G (making a fake frown): "Not quite. It means training your mind trains your body, and training your body trains your mind. It goes both ways. So how can you apply all of your training to your debate against Dylan?"

Me: "I'm not going to actually fight Dylan!"

Auntie G: "No, of course you aren't! Not with your body, anyway. But you are going to fight him with your mind."

And that's when we came up with the plan.

Dylan, you'd better bring your "A" game.

MONDAY, JUNE 22

*
* Two Days Until *
* Superhero Slam *
*

YIKES.

Just found out we're having a special assembly for the final of the Superhero Slam. I have to TALK in FRONT of the ENTIRE school! And the whole school will vote on the winner!

Ms. King came in all excited and thinks it's "amazing." I did not find it that amazing.

Despite what I wrote earlier about getting more comfortable, I'm already pretty nervous about going head to head with Dylan.

So I took a big breath. Just like on the TV shows and movies when somebody is about to do something BIG.

Just like Hayley Wickenheiser before stepping onto home ice for the Vancouver Olympics.

Just like Jessica Watson when she headed out to sea to begin her voyage around the world.

Just like Bryan Q. Miller when he decided which way to take his career.

Just like Nicole Stott the first time she stepped onto the International Space Station.

Just like Mike Bruen when he had to talk to his men about 9/11.

Just like Yuriko Romer before she started filming.

Just like Clara Hughes when she decided to simply talk openly about her depression so she could help other people.

Just like Kelly Sue DeConnick when she began to write stories for Captain Marvel and the Avengers.

I'm the new and improved Jessie.

I am Batgirl in the Superhero Slam.

This isn't going to be easy. But I can do this. I will do this.

I.

Will.

Do.

This.

☺

TUESDAY, JUNE 23

Now when I see Cade and Audrey together, I realize I should have seen their relationship coming. I mean here I have been training my "powers of observation" but I did not realize that Audrey's crushing on Cade. And she's been crushing for a while. It seems. Why didn't I notice? Anyway, she hid it pretty well. Which is pretty amazing, since she is so bad at lying.

Although, I never actually came right out and asked her if she liked Cade as more than a friend. You know, "Hey Audrey, are you crushing on Cade?" is something I just never thought to ask, actually.

It just shows that you can prepare all you want, but there are always going to be surprises.

Superheroes know they just have to deal with it.

WEDNESDAY, JUNE 24

* Superhero Slam Final! *

Today was it. The final of the Superhero Slam. Me versus Dylan. Batgirl versus Batman. Girl versus boy. Nervous versus whatever Dylan was. He had his hoodie pulled up so tight I couldn't see his face. He was standing there looking kind of relaxed but arrogant, if that's possible.

236

Could Batgirl finally beat Batman?

I was sweating it. I was so freaked out that Ms. King would pull out "critical thinking" and I would be doomed!

But Ms. King had one final twist for both of us. Ms. King said for the final we would use a slightly different format. We would each first explain why our hero was the best. What?! How awesome! I was so relieved about not having to face my fear about "critical thinking" that I forgot to be nervous!

Good thing too, because I went first. I figured Dylan would go the fighting route with me because he thinks Batman, as a man, could physically defeat Batgirl. So I was prepared! I talked all about evasiveness, use of everything and everyone around me, being agile and mobile. Basically all of what Auntie G taught me.

Dylan made good points about using critical thinking to find solutions to problems and that Batman recovered from losing his parents and used this to fire and fuel his determination.

> Me ("Pow!"): "History has shown us that agility and the ability to constantly adapt are the secrets to success. It's called EVOLUTION! Batgirl has had to evolve over her entire career. To change according to what was needed. And she's always been successful."

Not totally sure, but I think I caught a glimpse of Mr. Richardson doing a fist bump with Mr. Pratt when I said "evolution."

> Dylan ("Bang!"): "Batman is an original. He's actually THE original self-made superhero. Batman is the grandfather of superheroes. As a teacher and mentor to Batgirl, he'd know not only her strengths, but also her weaknesses. And he'd use those weaknesses to defeat her."

Dylan's lead was pretty good, actually. And he kind of ignored my points and just went with his strong stuff. He did a lot of homework, for sure. He also praised Batgirl a lot, which I didn't expect. But there was a lot that happened today that I didn't expect. It turns out it was kind of a setup. So I had to think fast.

> Me ("Biff!"): "Batgirl has had to fight and fight and fight her whole career. Fighting bad guys who are bigger, fighting against those who said a woman couldn't be a superhero, fighting for

her friends and for society. Having to repeatedly
face weakness helps make Batgirl strong. Only
by fully learning what her limits are could Batgirl
overcome her limits and defeat Batman. Batgirl's
had to deal with more hardship than Batman.
With all her hardship comes more toughening up,
like a hand constantly being slammed against a
tree!"

Dylan ("Wham!"): "Fair enough that Batman
hasn't had to struggle with stereotypes. But he
has struggled against the odds his whole career.
And he's been a champion the whole way. He has
too much experience to fall to Batgirl."

Me ("Kapow! BIFF! BAM! BOOM!"): "Batman is a
true teacher who wants his students to do well.
In fact, to do BETTER THAN HE DID. So, Batgirl
would know his real limits too. He would have
taught her how to beat someone like him. And
who would know better how to beat Batman than
Batman?"

Then it was the final minute of the Superhero Slam.
One whole year of preparation boiled down to this last
minute! It was straight out of an epic comic book!

Ms. King switched on her microphone to tell us that
there was one final surprise attribute we'd have
to debate. I'm not sure I could even feel individual
heartbeats anymore. My heart was pounding so fast it
was one giant BOOM!

The final attribute?

Ms. King turned to us and asked, "How is your superhero better at teamwork and collaboration?"

Since I went first in the normal round, Dylan led off here.

It gave me time for one more calming deep breath. Which I did while slowly stepping away from the microphone and closing my eyes. But I did peek once into the crowd to see Cade and Audrey staring up at me. Audrey had a little grin on.

And then we were back at it . . .

> Dylan: "Batman is the ultimate team player. He's been in the Justice League forever. He's been in Batman and the Outsiders; he's trained Robin, Nightwing, Spoiler, and tons of others. Superman comes to him for advice. Wonder Woman asks him things. Batman. Trained. Batgirl. Student does not beat teacher."

And suddenly something I should have noticed all along hit me like a smack on the forehead. Who has been a product of teamwork and collaboration more than me this entire school year?

I've had help from Ricki, from Mom, from Dad, Auntie G, Cade, Audrey, Shay, all the people I interviewed . . . even Dylan helped me by being someone for me to focus on!

So, who's more ready and prepared to answer about teamwork and collaboration than me and my superhero Batgirl?

No one. That's who.

I took another calming deep breath but this time I stepped up to the microphone and looked out at the whole crowd. I could see Dylan out of the corner of my eye. He didn't look like a superhero. Not even like a supervillain. He just looked like a nervous kid.

Me: "Batgirl works with others. She's a leader but she's first among equals. She's been in lots of teams like Birds of Prey. She's worked with Robin, Nightwing, and Batman. The key is she works WITH everyone. She understands everyone has their own strengths and that putting all those individual strengths together creates the most powerful thing ever. Batgirl is THE team player and that makes her the greatest superhero. EVER!"

And then something happened I could never have prepared for.

Dylan gave up.

He actually said into the microphone, in front of everyone: "I give up!"

Yes, that was actually it. He gave up. He conceded that Batgirl could beat Batman! This took everybody by surprise, me most of all.

When Dylan said that, the gym got really quiet. Then Ms. King took over, counting hands as she called out for those voting for Batman and then Batgirl. All of this was a blur to me as Dylan and I both sat back in our seats.

So, could Batgirl beat Batman? YES! She could and she did. I worked hard on this project and grew a lot. It was awesome – I was awesome!

It was also terrifying. I tried really hard to avoid looking at the whole school gathered in the gym watching us.

But then I saw lots of happy faces — most importantly Cade and Audrey jumping up and down and hugging in the front row. I even noticed Dylan looking over at me. But not with an angry stare or a mad glare because he'd lost.

Instead Dylan had a kind of small smile on his face. And then he nodded.

Which was kind of weird. What's up with that?

I won as Batgirl because of her ability to work with others and therefore think of others. For Batgirl, it's not all about her. Batman in Dylan's hands was just about fighting and doing his own thing.

I'm exhausted now despite how great it feels to win the Superhero Slam. It was quite frightening being up on that stage in the final. But I felt like I was in the zone up there. Like I do when I'm training with Auntie G. Totally focused on what I am doing and nothing else.

I am very happy that my inner Batgirl showed herself after all.

Turns out my inner Batgirl is really just me.

And that's more than enough for me.

THURSDAY, JUNE 25

This is my final interview for this diary. I got my reply from science journalist Christie Nicholson. She's a contributing editor at SCIENTIFIC AMERICAN and has written articles about all kinds of things — including science and superheroes!

Hi Christie,

My friend Audrey and I have read lots of your work. We really like how you make science articles so interesting. Audrey is full-on going to be an awesome scientist, engineer, inventor, or something when she gets older. And I'm into your articles because I like asking questions, getting answers, and writing.

You guessed it — I want to be a journalist one day. (Maybe even a science journalist so I can keep tabs on Audrey.)

As part of a school project, I've been researching about training the body and if a girl could become Batgirl with enough time, effort, and work. And enough food. (Seriously, you get super hungry from all that training.) I've written to a lot of really cool people about it. But I haven't written to anyone to ask about the actual thing I'm doing — being a journalist!

That's why I'm writing you. I have some questions I hope you'll answer!

* Do you have to read up a lot on something before you interview somebody?
* How do you get your ideas for what to write about?
* How and why did you get into journalism in the first place?
* What's the coolest part of your job? The least cool (I was going to write "suckiest" but I'm pretty sure that isn't a word)?

* Do you have a favorite superhero? (It's okay if you don't, but this is kind of my "signature question.")

Thank you so much!
Jessie

Hi Jessie!

Thanks for reaching out to me. I am very excited about your project—I'd like to see the outcome, as I'm curious how an ordinary human can become an extraordinary superhero.

I guess that is the number-one characteristic nearly all journalists share: a curiosity for pretty much everything. And it appears you have it!

So to answer your questions about being a journalist . . .

I decided to become a journalist because I love sharing information with others. I especially love watching another person enjoy and react to fascinating stories—hopefully sparking a conversation that might enlighten all involved.

Before I interview any source (the people I go to for information or a story), I absolutely read and learn about them and the subject I'm writing about. Often I do most of this research on the web, reading through past newspaper and magazine articles and blog posts. I want to find out the latest news on my topic, so that I know what new angle I can provide for my readers.

Finding a good idea is one of the tougher parts of a journalist's job. I sometimes find ideas in other articles, but it's important to put a new spin or "take" on a subject. The best ideas, however, come from talking with people. What you are looking for is something interesting, new, and relevant. For this we have to trust ourselves . . . meaning if you find something interesting, it's likely others will find it interesting too. So as a journalist, I always stop and take note of anything that catches my interest and see if I could turn it into a story that might be relevant for my specific audience.

For me, the coolest part of the job is having an excuse to call up amazing scientists and have long conversations with them. Having access to great thinkers and learning about their work is such a pleasure.

The toughest part of the job is taking all the research and interviews and organizing it to create an engaging and important story. This is by far the hardest thing for me.

On the superhero question—hmm, I guess my favorite superhero is Iron Man. I've always been a fan of inventors and I see Iron Man as the most innovative. Plus he seems like he might be a cool person to hang out with.

Good luck, Jessie, with your Batgirl project and your pursuit of a career in journalism. For me it's been great fun.

All the best,
Christie

All my research has really strengthened my journalism
skills! Journalists can be like superheroes because
they can get themselves in (and out of!) dangerous
situations, have to have critical thinking skills, have
to be brave, and have to expose the truth. No matter
what.

Something else, too. When Audrey finally finishes
off her exoskeleton project (all that stuff with Cade
side-tracked her), I'm going to ask Christie about
interviewing her!

FRIDAY, JUNE 26

Today was the last day of grade 8, the last day of,
well, all of middle school. So it was sure a different kind
of day. People saying goodbye like always at the end of
the year.

But also not like always because there are, like, five different high schools we are all off to. Luckily, Audrey, Cade, and I are going to the same one — the one that's been right outside my backyard for the past 10 years!

It has a great writing program and a really good arts program. Including photography! Which would really help with my journalism career. When I told Dad that's the one I wanted to go to, he was like, "Finally, you can walk to school!" Which I think means "Finally, I don't have to drive you to school when you miss your bus."

But some of us are going off to other schools. Like Dylan, for example. He is going to a school with a basketball academy program. At one point (actually at many points) this year, knowing he was going to a different high school would have made me happy. But it's weird to think I won't see him around anymore.

I started off this diary in September wondering (or being forced to wonder) what I had inside. What I was capable of. Basically, who was I?

I still don't know for sure. But I do know I feel pretty good about what I could do. And can do. What the possibilities are. Not sure if I really want to become a superhero like Batgirl. (And not just because of what Hayley Wickenheiser said about the costume! Too funny.)

But I do know a lot more about the work and effort needed to do something big. All the people I wrote to this year told me that.

So for my big diary finale here's my list of the Top 10

Things I Learned From My Interviews. In random order!

* "I don't think you have to have superpowers to achieve amazing things; we can all do amazing things if we believe in ourselves!"
—Jessica Watson

* "Do you ever defeat fears or do you just get used to them?? Well, I guess a little of both. There is no substitute for training and the other side of that is there is REALLY no substitute for actually doing." —Mike Bruen

* "I have a real live superhero and that is my mom. She is superhuman to me!" —Clara Hughes

* "You should never go to a place of 'a girl wouldn't say that!' Anyone, of any race, of any sex, can do or say anything. How they behave is based on their past experiences and their current sense of self." —Bryan Q. Miller

* "What's best for us is who we are. Each of our challenges is unique and we are uniquely qualified to live our lives our 'best.'"
—Kelly Sue DeConnick

* "I believe that you should always go after your dreams, no matter how high or how hard they seem — that just makes you try harder!"
—Hayley Wickenheiser

* "Today I look around and I see many real women superheroes! I hope we keep adding more and more women to our list of

superheroes." —Yuriko Romer

* "We did so much training so we could respond to things we could control if something did happen" —Nicole Stott

* "We have to trust ourselves."
  —Christie Nicholson

* "There's a superhero in you." —Jessie (That's me. I needed one more to make 10. And I learned this year that this is true. ☺)

I'm going to make a big mural of this for my wall!

But . . . later. Time to start my vacation with a little rest and relaxation!

Right after I clean my room.

Even superheroes have to do chores.

Apparently.

ACKNOWLEDGMENTS

The genesis of this book, a hybrid fiction and non-fiction project following a school year in the life of Jessie, was the direct result of the conversations I've had with thousands of people aged 10 to 16. I've done many, many talks and presentations about my first two books, *Becoming Batman* and *Inventing Iron Man*. A lot have been in elementary, middle, and high schools. By far the majority have been with middle schools and grades 6 to 8.

Some time ago, I started to think about writing a book specifically for a younger age group. In a way, *Project Superhero* is the answer to questions like: "Have you thought about writing a book for tweens?" or "Would you ever write something about female superheroes?" Another obvious question is "If you do write a book for teens, would you illustrate it? But not using your own drawings (which are terrible), but instead with an amazingly gifted artist who has made amazing animated movies?" (OK. That last question wasn't one I was ever asked. But it is true that my drawings *would* be terrible, and Kris Pearn, the illustrator, *is* an amazingly gifted artist.) *Project Superhero* is for everyone I've met and for all those out there wondering about who they can be. It's a book about a young and inquisitive teen trying to find out about herself through her love of friends, superheroes, science, and writing.

I've been very fortunate that many amazing people have allowed me to interview them and ask them the questions Jessie needs answered. Jessie gives special thanks to: Mike Bruen, retired NYPD sergeant on duty at Ground Zero for 9/11; Kelly Sue DeConnick, comic book writer for *Captain Marvel* and *Avengers Assemble*; Clara Hughes, Canadian six-time Winter and Summer Olympic medalist in speed skating and cycling and mental health spokesperson; Bryan Q. Miller, writer for *Batgirl* and *Smallville*; Christie Nicholson, contributing editor, *Scientific American* and *SmartPlanet*; Yuriko Romer, filmmaker (*Mrs. Judo: Be Strong, Be Gentle, Be Beautiful*) who documented the life of Keiko Fukuda—the highest ranking woman in judo history; Nicole Stott, NASA astronaut who spent more than three months on the International Space Station and has been in space six times; Jessica Watson, author of *True Spirit: The True Story of a 16-Year-Old Australian Who Sailed Solo, Nonstop, and Unassisted Around the World*; Hayley Wickenheiser, Olympic gold medalist and World Champion in ice hockey and community advocate for girls in sport.

I would also like to thank my agents Sam Hiyate and Alison MacDonald (for her Batgirl level of energy and insight), Stephanie Carmichael, Maiya MacMaster, Chelsea Kaupp, Yao Sun, Kate Scarth, and Rachael Renda for comments on earlier drafts of this book. Thanks to Jack David and ECW Press for taking a chance on an unusual idea. Many thanks also to Patricia Ocampo whose editorial insights made a superheroic contribution to the flow and organization of the book! Thanks also to the organizers of TEDx Edmonton 2012. It was at this event that Kris and I met and the beginnings of our collaboration took root.

In creating this book, I tried to write using the voice of all those I've spoken with in my own journey as an author. I hope I hit the right notes and that you enjoyed Jessie's grade 8 year!

E. Paul Zehr, a professor at the University of Victoria, is the author of *Becoming Batman* (2008) and *Inventing Iron Man* (2011), and he writes for *Psychology Today* and *Scientific American*. Veteran animation story artist of *Open Season*, *Surf's Up*, *Arthur Christmas* and *Cloudy With a Chance of Meatballs*, Kris Pearn co-directed 2013's *Cloudy With a Chance of Meatballs 2*.

To learn more about Jessie
and your inner superhero, go to
ProjectSuperhero.ca!

Get the eBook Free!